Praise for *Gabe Johnson Takes Over*

"A funny, uplifting, and rousing book that'll make readers think. In other words, it's a real gem."

—K. M. Walton, author of *Cracked and Empty*

"The funny, profane text embraces the idea that nobody is perfect. Gabe's character growth will satisfy any appetite. A funny popcorn read."

—*Kirkus*

"Geoff Herbach proved with his debut novel, *Stupid Fast*, that he could tap into the mind of a teen on the periphery. Herbach delivers another funny, poignant novel about an unlikely hero."

—*Shelf Awareness*

"Told in the first-person voice that Geoff Herbach does so well, Gabe Johnson's account of his development of the 'leadership bone' is grand, touching, and hilarious."

—*Star Tribune*

Also by Geoff Herbach

Stupid Fast

Nothing Special

I'm With Stupid

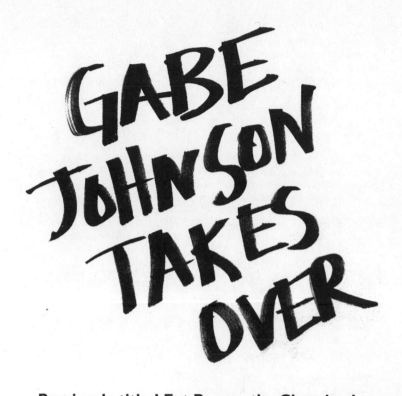

GABE JOHNSON TAKES OVER

Previously titled Fat Boy vs. the Cheerleaders

BY
GEOFF
HERBACH

sourcebooks
fire

Published by Sourcebooks Fire, an imprint of Sourcebooks, Inc.
P.O. Box 4410, Naperville, Illinois 60567-4410
(630) 961-3900
Fax: (630) 961-2168
www.sourcebooks.com

Library of Congress Cataloging-in-Publication Data

Herbach, Geoff.
   [Fat Boy vs. the cheerleaders.]
   Gabe Johnson takes over / Geoff Herbach.
     pages cm
   Summary: When the high school cheerleading team takes over a soda vending machine's funds, which were previously collected by the pep band, Gabe Johnson, an overweight "band geek" tired of being called names and looked down on, declares war.
   (13 : alk. paper) [1. Overweight persons--Fiction. 2. Protest movements--Fiction. 3. Cheerleading--Fiction. 4. Bands (Music)--Fiction. 5. High schools--Fiction. 6. Schools--Fiction. 7. Family life--Minnesota--Fiction. 8. Minnesota--Fiction.] I. Title.
   PZ7.H417Gab 2015
   [Fic]--dc23
                        2014040485

Printed and bound in the United States of America.
VP 10 9 8 7 6 5 4 3 2 1

For Mira and Leo

MEMORANDUM

From: Henry P. Rodriguez, Attorney at Law

Submitted To: Seventh District Court, Otter County

Re: Case No. 1745321—Gardener et al. v. MLA Independent School District

Shortly before midnight on June 15, Gabriel Johnson, a sixteen-year-old from Minnekota, MN, was apprehended outside Cub Foods by Officer Rex McCoy. Johnson possessed $17.75 in small bills and change, which he confirmed had been removed from the vending machine at Minnekota Lake Area High School.

Police suggested the alleged robbery was related to a larger conflict involving assault, vandalism, and defamation of character that has come to be known as the Spunk River War.

The following transcript is Gabriel's verbatim account, recorded in a conference room at the Minnekota police department between 10 a.m. and 5:40 p.m. on June 16.

We submit this document as context for the

above noted case. There is a specific human cost when those in power wield power arrogantly. This case supports a teenager's fight for dignity, opportunity, and fairness.

CHAPTER 1

Ripping off the pop machine last night wasn't meant to be funny. It was my duty to all the geeks, burners, and oddballs in school because that machine sucks. Robbing it was serious business, okay?

Why are you laughing, Mr. Rodriguez?

I did it myself. I robbed the machine all by myself.

There were sheep in the school this morning? Real sheep?

How—Oh, wait, I remember now. I must've let them in there by accident. Whoops. Like…left the door open after I robbed the machine and all those sheep wandered in by themselves.

No, it's not funny, sir. Really.

I'm telling you I'm the one who stole the money. It was eighteen dollars, but I lost a quarter when Officer McCoy roughed me up. Look at my chin! I have scrapes all over my stomach and knees too.

That stupid pop machine. Stupid pop. It all started with that stupid—

Yeah, I hate that machine. For so many reasons.

First things first! That machine made me a junky! A pop junky! I'm not the only one in school either.

Back in May, me, Justin Cornell, and Camille Gardener did this pop study for health class. It was Camille's idea because she turned into a health nut when her dad started organic farming last year. (Her dad grew like two tomatoes and one giant zucchini. Mr. Gardener's not the greatest farmer in the world.) Anyway, out of Camille's concern for health, she got us to study usage of the pop machine, her theory being that unhealthy kids would be the heaviest users.

Big, bad study, sir.

Mr. Luken, our health teacher, gave us passes to hang out in the cafeteria all day. We made a chart of jocks, brains, music geeks, gamers, burners, and others (sad sacks who are hard to categorize because they have no social connections to anyone) and we took note of who purchased a product from the pop machine and what specific product they purchased.

Almost nobody paid attention to us while we took

notes. Only a couple said stuff like, "What are you staring at, dorks?" Seth Sellers, a jock, made fart sounds when he saw me.

This pop project was eye opening, sir.

After school that day, me, Camille, and Justin went to Bitterroot Coffee Shop down on Main Street to tally things up.

"Nick, *Gamer*, purchased three Pepsis in four hours," Justin said.

"Kendra, *Burner*, four different pops in five hours," Camille said.

"She's pretty overweight," Justin said.

"Not as big as Tiff, *Other*, who bought four bottles of Sierra Mist," Camille said.

"Oh, Lord Mother of all Balls," I said.

Camille plugged the data into a spreadsheet, squinting.

Justin shook his head, sucked his latte, and was all like, "Whoa."

Then Camille sat back, sipped her green tea, and was all like, "Just as I suspected."

I smiled and said, "Holy Mother of all Balls, right?" I drank a mocha with whipped cream, which has a million calories by the way.

Here's the scoop, sir: Purchasers of pop at Minnekota Lake Area High School are fat asses, trailer park kids, addicted gamers, and burner chicks who eat cigarettes for breakfast. Dozens and dozens of these kids. Most of them went for seconds later in the day. Some for thirds. A couple fourths (me, for instance). Very few jocks purchased pop from the machine. (Seth Sellers bought one bottle of Pepsi late in the afternoon, so he was able to greet me with the aforementioned fart sounds.) Two cheerleaders purchased from the machine, but they both bought diet. That diet stuff will kill you but not make you fat on the calories.

What does that tell you, Mr. Rodriguez?

I tried not to show my concern, but Justin and Camille were clearly concerned.

"You drink a lot of pop, Chunk," Justin said. "Could be part of the problem,"

"Oh, is there a problem?" I said. "I wasn't aware of a problem!" I smiled big and raised my fat mocha like I was making a toast.

"There's a problem, Chunk," Camille said. "A big problem." She didn't smile. She didn't toast me.

"I'm just sayin'," Justin said.

Yeah. Really. A problem. I drank a hell-ton of Code Red Mountain Dew every day—four bottles, five bottles—and the only pants that fit me were stretchy pants (elastic waistband, sir).

I knew it too, knew pop was part of my issue. But see, I also thought it was part of my success. I was winning by buying all that pop! All the vending machine money went to fund the band! I'm a trombone player, you know? That's one badass, hilarious instrument, right? Trombone! Awesome instrument. I love band so much, so I figured I was paying myself by drinking all that pop. Winning it huge.

No. Stupid.

The truth is, I've gained a load of weight in the last couple years. Kids call me fat ass, sausages, fudge balls, butter balls, cake balls, lard ass, Eight-Butt Johnson. All kinds of names. I laugh and go along with it, but those names hurt my feelings.

Even my stupid gym teacher calls me names!

The day after our pop study, I was depressed, so it took me a long time to get to school. So I was late to gym class. So Mr. McCartney ordered me to "orbit," which means run laps. I didn't want to get detention. (McCartney had been threatening me with detention because I make jokes and I'm quote unquote *mouthy*.) So I did what I was told.

While I was jogging around the gym, Seth Sellers shouted, "Planet turd in orbit!"

I smiled. "Yeah, watch out, planet Earth. This shit ball might crash out of the night sky!" I faked being out of control and weaved off course like I was crashing.

McCartney got pissed. "This isn't a joke, Chunk," he said. "This is a punishment."

"Okay," I said. "Sorry." I jogged on, but when I got to the far end of the gym, Janessa Rogers, this nasty cheerleader, said, "Shake it, Chunk! Shake it!"

I puckered my lips duckface style and started shaking my ass while I jogged.

Everybody laughed.

Everybody except McCartney. He freaked. Way out of control. His face turned dark red and sweat streamed down his forehead. He started yelling, "You wanna be a clown, Chunk? You wanna disrupt my class? Oh, you're real hilarious!"

I stopped ass-shaking.

"God, I'm sick of it," McCartney shouted.

I stopped jogging altogether. Stared at him because he was screaming. Everyone else stopped whacking their birds. (We were in a badminton unit.)

McCartney walked toward me fast. "I'm so sick of your baloney. Sick of your face."

"My face?" I asked because I was surprised, because I always thought McCartney sort of liked me, even if I annoyed him.

"Your fat face! Get out of my gym, you sack of shit. Get your fat ass out of here."

Everybody stared. Everybody's mouth hung open.

I swallowed hard. Stared at McCartney for a second. Then said, "Okay." I put my head down and bumbled out of there as fast as my fat legs could carry me.

Terrible. Teacher verbally assaults you like that?

Hey. Why are we talking about this, Mr. Rodriguez? Shouldn't we be talking about how…how you're going to keep me from going to jail or something? I'm a little nervous about my crime.

The whole story, huh? Okay. You asked for it. I can talk forever.

Pop. The night after I was kicked out of gym, I pulled

five empty bottles of Code Red Mountain Dew out of my backpack. (There isn't recycling at school, so I bring my empties home.) One bottle didn't have a cap on it. A little Code Red dribbled out onto my bedroom rug. It made a little stain. I squinted at it and my heart beat hard.

This stain reminded me of Doris, our cleaning lady, back when Dad was trying to pick up the pieces after Mom hit the road. (Mom ran away to Japan while I was in eighth grade by the way.)

Doris was a tiny old lady. She spilled dirty mop water on the carpet. She said, "Better laugh than cry." She broke a lamp when she whacked it off a side table with the duster. "Better laugh than cry."

Poor Doris! She was terrible. She could barely lift a broom she was so old. Dad had to fire her, which made him cry (serious sobbing breakdown, which he did a lot back then), but what was he going to do? She plugged the toilet with Clorox wipes. She broke a whole set of plates. She fell off a stool and ripped down our shower curtain. Dad had no choice. But when the taxi dropped her off at our place on the day he actually fired her, he broke down like a weak-ass baby. "I'm sorry," he cried. "I'm so sorry, Doris."

Doris shrugged and smiled and put her coat back on. I was so nervous about how she would react. What if Doris cried about getting fired? What would we do then? But she didn't seem to care at all. "Better laugh than cry," she said. Then Dad drove her home.

And I exhaled. I relaxed. And I thought, *Doris has it right, right? Better laugh than cry. I don't want to be a fool-sobbing mess like my dumb dad, who can't deal with his wife leaving him.* (My mom left me too and I wanted to cry—but seriously, *Better laugh than cry.*) That became my whole way of dealing.

A couple years later, there I was, ass-dancing in the high school hallway while Seth Sellers mocked me with fart sounds. Laughing all the way, man.

But that night, I stared at that Code Red stain on my rug and my heart beat. And I thought, *That's not funny.* For the first time, sir, it occurred to me that my total lack of dignity is not remotely funny.

That feeling continued into the night.

Grandpa, who you met this morning, moved in with me and Dad last summer to help us out. He cooks really well and sort of cleans—better than Doris, I guess. After he got too old to be a professional bodybuilder,

Grandpa ran a diner in town and the dude can make comfort food like nobody's business.

Yes, you heard me right—bodybuilder.

Why are you laughing?

Everybody in town knows about Grandpa. He was Mr. Minnesota 1977, Mr. Rodriguez. I'm serious. The ladies loved him. Grandpa was Arnold Schwarzenegger's main competition back in the day.

That's what he told me and I believe him.

Long story short, sir, that night, Grandpa cooked up some steaks and a bunch of mushrooms in butter sauce and mashed potatoes and green beans and fixed us salads. The deal is, I never ate the green beans or the salad part. I doubled up on mashed potatoes because oh, balls, yes, do I love the awesome flavor of my grandpa's cream cheese–infused mashed potatoes.

While I was sucking down the potatoes, Grandpa stared at me. He said, "Boy, the lack of roughage in your diet accounts for that big gut of yours."

I looked up, stared back at Grandpa's pinched face. I remembered Mr. McCartney calling me a fat ass in gym. My heart sank. My chin quivered. "Big gut?" I asked.

"You heard me," he said.

I swallowed hard, thought I might cry because of all these names. But then my Doris philosophy kicked in. I said, "I'm out of here!" I put the rest of the potatoes in my mouth—a giant wad—jumped up from my chair and ass-danced out of the dining room.

"Sure love the spuds, don't ya, ya Chunk?" Grandpa called after me.

"Ha-ha!" my dad laughed.

Back downstairs in my room, I stared at the stain again. *What the hell is so funny? Am I really just a joke?* I pictured Doris's quivery arms and unsteady gaze and her wrinkled old face.

Then it hit me! *Oh, man*, I thought. *Crap! You're not Doris, you idiot.*

Total realization, sir. Doris couldn't help it that she was so old. What was she going to do? Cry about living so long she no longer had control of her body? Better laugh than cry makes sense for her. I, on the other hand, have a choice. I'm a powerful young buck. Ass-dancing isn't the only option, right?

Don't get me wrong, sir. I like being funny. But I don't like—

You asked for it! The whole story! This totally has to do with the pop machine.

See, I was already pretty crabby that last week of school. Because I tried to limit my Code Red intake to three bottles a day, because I didn't want to be a victim anymore, didn't want to just laugh it all off. I wanted to do something for myself. I'd become dependent on the sugar and caffeine in the freaking pop, okay?

Justin and Camille both commented on my bad mood.

"Why so sad?" Justin asked while he was driving me to school.

"Someone hit you with the sad stick?" Camille asked during chemistry.

"Bah," I replied to both of them. "Screw everything."

See? I was already evolving the attitude that caused me to become the criminal I am today.

Then Wednesday that last week of school, we had the first tiny event of what has since come to be known as the Spunk River War.

What a stupid name. Spunk. That's a bonehead name.

Sure thing, sir. Go ahead and get coffee. I'll be here when you get back. Not like I can go anywhere.

CHAPTER 2

Styrofoam cup, sir? Why do these places still have
Styrofoam? It's bad for the environment.

No, I don't hate you for drinking the coffee. I just
wonder, Mr. Rodriguez.

Okay. So Wednesday morning. Four dollars and
fifty cents jangled in my stretchy pants pocket. Just
enough for three bottles of Code Red. (I was keeping
myself in check—no extra money so I wasn't tempted
to go for more.) Maybe I was crabby, but I felt good
about the fact I was trying.

And then—totally evil surprise. Parched, ready for
my first Dew of the day, I strolled into the cafeteria and
discovered that all pops in our pop machine had been
jacked from a buck fifty to $2.25! No longer did I have
the proper coinage for three Code Reds. I only had
enough for two. I couldn't make it through a school
day on two Code Reds! *Oh, no, no—*

By lunch, I was swimming in the swamp of despair. Sick in my heart, sir. I finished my second and last Code Red of the day and looked down at my empty tray (school-quality corn dog already sucked into my belly).

Camille said, "Chunk, what's your damage? You're not remotely funny these days."

"I got nothing," I mumbled.

"Seriously, what's going on?" Justin asked. "You're on a downward slide, man."

Although it wasn't the only problem, it was the problem of the day. I pointed at the pop machine and whispered, "Pop price."

"Are you kidding?" Camille asked.

"No."

"Really?" Justin said. "The price of pop has knocked you on your ass?"

"Yes. Unfair business practices," I mumbled.

"How so?" Justin asked. "Prices are determined by the market. Look. Chandra Gore is up there buying pop right now. The market will bear the higher price."

I looked over and watched Chandra Gore (one of the "sad sacks" in our health class project) pull a bottle of lemonade from the machine. Her real last name isn't

Gore. It's Wettlinger, but Wettlinger isn't goth enough for her, so we call her Gore. She tries to look like hell. (I know now that she's beautiful, sir, so beautiful.) She wants to be scary (all bleeding black eyeliner and makeup that makes her look pale and dead).

"So? What about competition?" I asked. "Where's the competition? There's only one pop machine in here, owned by one company that sets the price. No competition."

Justin cocked his eyebrow, which has always been his way of saying, *Dude, you are an idiot.*

But Camille agreed. "I don't believe we should have all these sugary drinks for sale in a school, but as long as we do, Chunk really has a point."

"I suppose there's a lack of competition," Justin said. "But the profits do go to the band program and bands aren't cheap. Isn't it reasonable that we pay a premium for pop to support the common good of the band?"

"Oh, yeah," Camille said. "Point Cornell."

"Stick it in your asses," I said.

"Whoa. Dude," Justin said.

"Stick what? A pop? Can I borrow a couple bucks so I can buy one?" Camille asked.

Justin laughed.

"Seriously. Stick it," I said.

"I'm just joking," Camille said.

"Keep your stupid jokes to yourself," I said.

"Will do," Camille whispered. Her face got red.

Justin squinted at me. He said, "Okay, Chunk. Let's talk to the principal. We should lodge a complaint at least. You're right. That's a pretty crazy price hike. What's wrong with a quarter? Just from our research, we know there are low-income kids who drink a ton of pop. They're probably doing that instead of eating breakfast. They have to be suffering from this."

Justin is class president, so he acts all powerful.

Camille nodded like she agreed but then left the table, probably because I hurt her feelings.

Justin made a plan for us to go to see Principal Deevers.

CHAPTER 3

Here's something I've recognized, Mr. Rodriguez: Even if you're a born leader, leading takes practice and discipline, and if you've spent two years sucking down hot dogs while ass-dancing, you sound like a buffoon in leadership situations. I did anyway. The leadership bone weakens when not used.

After school, Justin and I walked into the principal's office. Without my minimum three Code Reds, I was totally wiped and a little whacked, a bit confused, and my muscles felt like bags of sand.

We got past the turtleneck and pink sweater secretaries based on Justin's president cred and got in front of Mr. Deevers, sat down in his florescent light office.

He wasn't happy to see us. Why would a principal suffer discomfort at getting a visit from one of his top students and me, an inflatable boy who never causes harm but only brings joy? Maybe because he's a central figure in a scheme to defraud said students out of their hard-earned American dollars?

"What do you guys want?" he asked.

"Justice," I mumbled.

Justin raised his eyebrow, laughed. "We're just curious about the sudden steep price increase on the pop machine."

Deevers cleared his throat. "Happens. Inflation. Sorry," Deevers said. "Is that all?"

Justin got a little pissed. He's not used to educators acting dismissively toward him. "Did your costs rise by fifty percent? I doubt it. Why the need for extra cash?"

"Calm down, Justin," Deevers said. "All money is going back into programming. Come on. Times are tough for education. You know that. Property values are down all over the district. Fewer people visited Minnekota resorts the last few years. Tax revenues are…are lessening. Money is tight and we're depending on those proceeds to fund a lot."

"Fund more than just the band?" Justin asked.

Deevers smiled a fake smile. His eyes darkened. "Well, ha-ha, there will be an announcement tomorrow on that front. Ha-ha," he said.

I squinted, stared at that fake smile. "Ha-ha?" I asked. "What do you mean 'Ha-ha'?"

"I didn't say 'Ha-ha,'" Mr. Deevers said.

"Yes, you did. Ha-ha," I said.

Justin whispered, "Keep cool."

"Ha-ha. Wait for tomorrow. Big announcement," Deevers said.

"Ha-ha? Ha-ha?" I barked. "Are you taking my money? Are you running away to Mexico?" I cried.

"No, Chunk!" Deevers laughed. "Of course not."

"Jesus," Justin whispered.

"I don't have enough money to live!" I shouted.

"Time to go," Deevers said.

I was upset. Hugely so. I spent so much money on pop even before the price hike. My family doesn't have much money. I was so mad. But I was useless about it. Why didn't I say something about poor kids who don't eat breakfast at all, who need the caffeine even to have a fighting chance? Instead, I accused the principal of going to Mexico. I was an idiot. That's what I mean about a weak leadership bone. That's what I had.

We got out of the office and Justin walked away from me without saying a word.

The next day, I tried to hold it together by over-dosing on the Dew.

I went to the machine again and again. Six times in total. Almost fourteen bucks worth of Code Red in a day.

Oh, balls.

I need to confess something, sir. That's why you have me here, right? Confession? I might as well put it all on the table.

The money I earned working five hours a week at Dante's Donuts during the school year wasn't enough to pay for that much Dew at $2.25 a bottle. Please allow me to shed the ugly light on my stupid face, okay?

I robbed Grandpa of twenty bucks that morning. Plucked four five-dollar bills from his wallet while he fried eggs. Terrible. Part of the reason Grandpa lives with us is that he's poor. He invested all his money in this power drink made by one of his old buddies from back in his buff and oily bodybuilder days. It was called *Tiger Lightning* and it supposedly had the essence of tiger testicles in it. But it turned out the secret ingredient was actually a synthetic steroid and Grandpa's friend had his ass sued off by the government. And

Grandpa lost just about everything and there I am stealing from him? What a jerk.

But I was almost out of money and I couldn't take another day like the one before because I was weak and trembling and stupid all day. I don't want to be stupid. So I stole money and I poured that Code Red down my throat all morning. Too much Dew. At lunch, I was sweating, heart palpitating, probably on the cliff edge of overdosing. I couldn't concentrate. I could barely talk.

Camille said, "Gabe? Chunk? You okay?"

I nodded, but I was not okay.

Justin said, "Stop drinking that crap. You've got red dye all over your lips. You're freaking out."

I couldn't stop. The higher price made me want it more. I needed all the Code Red.

Scary. Have you ever noticed there's something about scarcity that drives people totally crazy? At least, it does for me. It happens at home too. Like, if Grandpa makes less mashed potatoes for dinner (sometimes he runs out of potatoes, so there's less), instead of peeling back, being reasonable, being a good member of my household (one that shares), I totally go wild. I dish out double my normal portion the first time around to keep Grandpa and Dad from eating a remotely normal amount. (I need mine!) This pisses them off, as it should.

"Hold on, buddy! That's hogging the trough!" Dad will say.

But I don't care. I can't care. The idea that I won't get my fill explodes in my heart, makes me desperate, and I explode all over those mashed potatoes. I jam them in my mouth as fast I as can in hopes I'll be able to scoop even more onto my plate before Dad and Grandpa want seconds.

When I get in that *Take it all now* mode, Dad says stuff like, "You're showing why democracy is bound to fail, Gabe. Somebody always wants more than their fair share and that someone is willing to forgo ethical considerations to get what they want."

(Dad should know. He hoards chips and chocolate in his closet.)

Then I'll say some crap like, "Capitalism is about winning, dude."

How messed up, right? Was I winning by downing untold gallons of Code Red? I stole from Grandpa! I poured money into that machine! My knees and back hurt all the time! I poured Code Red into my body, which made me want even more Code Red, which made me need more money and made me fatter! Sounds a lot like losing.

And—here's the real kick in the nuts—turns out that money I was spending wasn't even going to my band.

The next hour was study hall.

Justin, Camille, me, and a few others sat at a table in the cafeteria. They were all laughing and I'm usually the guy leading that. But I had my head down on the cold, stinky tabletop, my eyes closed. "Ha-ha!" I heard people laughing. "Ha-ha!"

Then there was silence. I looked up just as Kailey Kaus and the rest of the cheerleaders streamed into the room. We all stared. Kailey, Janessa Rogers, Emily Yu, and the rest put up posters all over. The posters had a picture of cheerleaders cheering on it. The headline read, *YES, THE RUMORS ARE TRUE!*

"Rumors?" Camille asked.

"This is the announcement Deevers was talking about yesterday," Justin said.

"What announcement?" Camille asked.

I stared at Kailey Kaus. Man, I always stared at Kailey Kaus. Forever.

Dad talked to you about her this morning, right, Mr. Rodriguez?

Let me admit this right now, sir: I used to love her. Used to. I don't now. I hate her now. She's my enemy.

Used to be different though. Back in elementary school, she lived in the house right behind mine, another crap ranch house. Her dad hadn't gotten rich yet. We went to Westlake Elementary, right on Minnekota Lake. Kailey's mom and my mom hung out. Kailey and I were more than best friends.

We were like a little husband and wife. We spent all our time together. I was Luke Skywalker and she was Princess Leia. ("Darth Vader is around that corner! Ah!"). I had a toy light saber. Her mom rolled her blond hair into those cinnamon bun things Leia has. We attacked the Death Star. ("We can do it!") We raised her doll babies together. ("Juniper has a runny nose, Luke. Get a Kleenex!") (I don't think we totally got that Luke and Leia are brother and sister.) We danced at the imaginary ball, celebrating our successful destruction of the Death Star. (Kailey's mom taught me to dance. She gave me lessons.) We were so close. Sometimes, during the summer after fifth grade, right before she moved across town, Kailey would knock on the basement rec room window at night. I'd slide out of that little slot and we'd run around in the dark, holding hands. We'd lie down in the dewy grass and look at the stars.

Amazing. I loved that.

There's this little girl who lives in Kailey's old house now. She plays on the back patio, reminds me of my love for Kailey.

But these days, Kailey is best friends with Janessa and Emily. Those girls want me to ass-dance. They don't know that the whole reason I learned to dance in the first place is because Kailey's mom was the teacher. Those girls laugh behind my back—but not so far behind me I can't hear them. I'm freaking Eight-Butt Johnson, man. I'm a fat, stupid joke to them.

Anyway, the poster.

YES, THE RUMORS ARE TRUE!

THANK YOU FOR SUPPORTING THE NEW DANCE SQUAD WITH YOUR POP PURCHASE!

All around "New Dance Squad," they had drawn

in hearts and stars and smiley faces. It made me want to puke.

"Holy balls," I whispered. "Oh, my God."

"This completely sucks," Camille said. "Doesn't the school board have to vote to fund something new?"

"I'm sure the school board did vote. We just didn't hear about it," Justin said. "It's no big deal."

That pissed me off, sir. "No big deal?" I said. I kicked back my chair, stood up. "This is fraud! I spent that money to help the band! We've been bamboozled!"

"Kailey's mom and dad have to be behind this," Camille said.

"Behind this? Behind what? A new school program? That's not exactly in the realm of conspiracy. Don't be so dramatic," Justin said. "Nobody's hiding anything."

"Uh, Kaus Company? The pop machine? They own it? The price went up?" Camille said. "Kailey's mom is head of the school board? Kailey is suddenly getting a dance team? Sounds like conspiracy to me."

"Drama," Justin said. "Just relax."

Here's the thing, sir. I did relax. "Oh," I sighed. I thought about Kailey knocking on my window the summer after fifth grade. "Crap," I said.

"Chunk's right," Camille shouted. "We've been bamboozled."

"Would you both please shut up?" I said quietly. I sat down, put my head back on the table.

"I'm getting kind of sick of your attitude," Justin said.

"Seriously, Chunk," Camille said.

"Whatever," I mumbled.

Terrible day, sir. It went on too. I didn't take a ride home from Justin after school. I left right as the bell rang and walked. Seth Sellers and Emily Yu pulled up next to me in Seth's car as I walked. "Hey, turd!" he shouted.

I stared straight forward, kept moving, didn't make any jokes.

They rolled along at my speed for about twenty seconds. They were expecting me to make an ass of myself, I'm sure. Then Seth shouted "Later, fat ass" and tore off.

Grandpa made lasagna that night. I ate a whole pan by myself.

"You doing okay, Chunk?" Grandpa asked.

Dad read his magazine.

"Fine," I said as I plowed through that lasagna.

Before school the next morning, the last morning because it was the last day of the year, I took a bunch of quarters from my dad's change mug. I wanted to drink all the Code Red in the world. I wanted to fill up and explode.

Hey. I have to go to the bathroom, Mr. Rodriguez.

CHAPTER 4

That bathroom is disgusting, sir.

Sure. Yeah. Serves its purpose. I'm good.

Where were we?

Right. Last day of school. That was nine days ago. Feels like a million years ago though. I stole money from Dad so I could drink all the Code Red in the world.

Actually, I tried not to go to school at all. After breakfast, instead of heading outside and down to the corner where Justin usually picks me up, I sat back down on the couch and shut my eyes.

By the time Grandpa noticed I hadn't left the house (and was asleep on the couch), I was too late to make gym (too late for Mr. McCartney to call me names one last time).

"What the hell?" Grandpa shouted when he saw me.

"Sick," I said, opening my eyes.

"No, you're not," Grandpa said. "Get in the van!"

Grandpa drove me to school in his dumb orange van, which I didn't appreciate.

Nobody seemed to notice or care that I'd skipped a class. I'm sure it would've been a big deal if it hadn't been the last day of school. I bought my first Dew and shuffled to second hour.

The morning was only notable for a couple reasons.

One, someone had stuffed a note in my locker saying, *I'm sorry, Gabe! I'm sorry. I'm sorry. I'm sorry!*

That's the note Dad handed you this morning, sir. Guess he found it when he was digging around my room last night. It's from Baba Obi and I don't have a clue why you guys think it has something to do with this pop machine robbery because it doesn't.

No, I don't know any Baba Obi.

The handwriting is a girl's. I'm sure Camille was sorry for something. It's nothing.

Baba Obi is no one.

Two, Ms. Feagan, my English teacher, asked me to stay after class following third hour. "Gabe, are you feeling all right?" she asked.

"No," I said. "I don't feel good."

"Do you need help? Can I help?"

"I just don't want to be funny anymore," I said.

She laughed for a second. "Okay," she said. "That's fair. You don't have to entertain me or anybody, but I've missed you this week."

"Sorry," I said.

"No," Ms. Feagan said. "Don't be sorry. You do what you need to do, okay?"

I nodded and left, but that meant a lot to me. Ms. Feagan is meritorious. (That's a vocabulary word from her class.)

Yeah, the morning was quiet. The afternoon wasn't.

Band changed everything.

Usually, the final day of band is a jam session. When I was a freshman, Mr. Shaver let us play our favorite songs of the year but also sort of improvise our parts, which was really hilarious. It was really, really great. Man, I love band. I love it, Mr. R. It's so fun. And Shaver is an awesome teacher and no one acts like a jerk or calls anyone names (well, except Austin Bates). We just play music. Some of it is boring, but lots of it is loud and bouncy sounding. It's so good. Last year, during the final day jam session, people got up and danced and whooped and crap. It was probably the best time I've ever had.

I'm serious, sir. I love band.

But this year, the last band class wasn't the jam session I was expecting at all, and clearly, I needed some joy in my life, right?

We all got to the band room and Mr. Shaver told us not to take our instruments out. He asked us to sit in our sections. His tone scared me. Dark.

Tess Cook, who is an airhead and maybe half deaf/crazy, didn't pay attention to instructions. She pulled out her clarinet and began to put it together and Mr. Shaver, who is about the sweetest dude in the world, flipped out. "Damn it, Tess. I said no instruments." The room fell totally silent. We all stared at Shaver. I had a hard time swallowing because his shouting freaked me out. He's not a yeller. He's a sweet old dude. (I mean, I thought he was until last week.)

Shaver got up on the riser, where he usually conducts. He said, "Big announcement. Big announcement. Sit down, Tess."

Tess was only up because she was putting her clarinet away. "What?" she asked. Her face turned red.

"Sit, kid. Jesus Christ," Shaver said. "Jesus!"

Tess sat with half her clarinet in her hand.

My hands were shaking by that point. I felt faint. (I'd already had five Code Reds, which likely added to my shaking.)

Then Shaver took this deep breath, shook his head, and delivered the blow. "I'm very sorry to say there will be no marching camp this summer."

There was an audible gasp. More like a hiss or a balloon losing air.

Someone—I'm not sure who—shouted, "Why?"

"Unforeseen circumstances," Shaver said. "Changes. Things come up. Get used to it. Things get in the way in life. You all enjoy your time off."

"Wait!" Camille shouted. "Seriously...why?"

But Shaver had already stepped down from the riser. While we watched, mouths hanging open, he walked across the room to his office, walked in, and slammed the door.

You might think the band would all riot or call out in anguish or something. Shouldn't we have pounded on Shaver's office, demanded an explanation, planned our resistance? No way. We all just sat there, barely breathing, waiting for Shaver to come back and further direct us about what we were supposed to do.

No leadership in the house.

The seniors were on their way out. It was their last day. They couldn't give a flying squirt about marching. The juniors who will be seniors are a class almost totally devoid of any intelligence or talent. It's like the smarts in this town skipped a generation. They can't play music. They can barely read. They're dirty and dumb.

Yes, I'm happy to say that some of them are my friends now.

But you have to have leaders if you're going to fight the power, man. Are sophomores who are used to being buried near the bottom of the shit heap going to be quick to stand up? Justin was the most likely dude to do it, but he didn't because he was already secretly dating Janessa.

That's right—Janessa Rogers!

People started whispering. The volume increased. They all talked and talked about what might've happened. *Maybe Shaver's sick. Maybe he's tired or he has to travel someplace. Maybe he doesn't like us anymore. Maybe the marching band is losing its funding for next year.*

Whoa. Stop the presses.

I hadn't partaken (partook?) in the conversations at all because of my state of mind, but—

Maybe the marching band is losing its funding for next year.

Okay, when I was a freshman, Jacinta Smith was the president of the student council, and she also took community college classes at night from my dad (accounting). And I actually read one of her papers where she talked about how various student activities were funded and the band, sir, the band's summer programming was entirely funded by proceeds generated from the pop machine in the cafeteria! I thought about Deevers telling me and Justin about property values and resort money and how there wasn't enough money.

I mean, balls!

Suddenly, I knew in my pounding heart of hearts what was going on. A high holy effenheimer danced on the tip of my tongue. I sucked it in and let it expand in my chest. My heart pounded, man.

Maybe the marching band is losing its funding for next year?

I tried to breathe. I tried to swallow. I watched and waited. Pretty soon, conversations turned to summer plans and college and all kinds of crap that didn't matter. Only I knew we were being victimized (totally bamboozled).

My blood boiled, not just for me but for all us geeks.

Look at me, Mr. Rodriguez. Here. I'm going to stand up. Do you think I like marching? I love the music—but marching? This is me marching. I look stupid, right? In fact, I hate the hell out of the marching part of band. The stupid tight pants and fur ball hats and the big white belt that crushes me across my midsection. I can't breathe in the bullshit uniform in the first place. Then march me around in circles while I blow my guts out on this brass instrument that requires all kinds of wind? I look like a dying blimp wearing a costume and blowing a big metal robot wang.

What I'm saying is while I love concert band and pep band with my whole heart, I don't like marching one bit. But I'd had enough of getting the shaft. I'm not a joke. I'm not going to be a victim!

Waiting for the bell to ring, I thought about Seth Sellers calling me a turd. I thought about the stinging price of Code Red and all the ways it crippled me (physically and emotionally). I thought about Deevers. I thought about the health class experiment and how

I wasn't the only one screwed over. I thought about McCartney and name-calling.

I thought, *None of this is by accident.* I thought, *Somebody is trying to use us up.* I thought, *If Kailey or Janessa were in the band, we'd have all the money we need to be the best band we can be. Property values and resort money don't matter! They take my stuff because I make it easy! I just laugh and roll over!*

I exhaled hard. I stood up. Everyone stared at me.

"I have totally and completely had enough of this bullshit," I said. "This means war!"

Austin Bates, a junior percussionist, laughed. "Ha-ha!"

I gave him the finger.

And then the bell rang.

CHAPTER 5

Mr. Rodriguez, have you ever felt the need to get a whole new set of friends? I'm not saying Justin and Camille are bad people. They're fine, okay? But Justin was the first person to call me Chunk instead of my given name, Gabe. (He said I looked like this fat kid in an 80s movie.) Camille treated me like an idiot all the time. And Justin "forgot" to give me a ride home that last day of school because clearly he had better things to do than deliver his best friend. That means something when you've decided to go to war.

I walked home. I cut through the school's playing fields and launched my last ever Code Red onto the track. It fizzled for a couple seconds and then died.

As I trudged through town, a little song established itself in my head, something like this: *What's a boy like me gonna do to fight? Who to beat to win victory? My eagle wings will take flight. I'll rain death and misery—*

Yeah, that's a bad song, sir. I sang it over and over.

I also thought about RC III, this dude who moved to Minnekota last fall. That guy's a fighter and also he doesn't treat me like an idiot. He was this superstar all-star Mr. Football and Basketball down in the Twin Cities the year before. But his dad—he's a lawyer who used to play for the Vikings—is working on that giant murder trial over in Green Lake, so RC III had to move here.

Right. Of course you've heard of him.

What a shock to his system, right? City schools and big shopping malls and all the movies you'd ever want to see and sophistication and people of many colors and nationalities and then you're here in the frozen lakes and bean fields with a bunch of blond kids staring at you like you're from Planet Zorb? Didn't seem to bother him at all.

Yeah, RC III kicked everybody's ass in the whole conference on the football field and the basketball court. It was a real joy to play my 'bone in the pep band this year because we actually won some games with RC III kicking ass like he did. What was really cool is that he didn't try to blend into the jock culture at all. Didn't try to become part of the school like that.

The dude was in my gym class this spring. For whatever reason, I was the only one he ever talked to. We'd pair up for badminton every day (if I wasn't orbiting or being kicked out of class).

I'd say, "Don't smash me in the shuttlecock."

He'd say, "I'm gonna smash your shuttlecock all over this gym, man."

Then he'd take it pretty easy on me and we'd whack the bird back and forth.

A couple times, though, he'd make it hard and I did okay. After class one time, he said, "You're pretty light on your feet for a big dude. You should get in shape and go out for football in the fall."

I said, "I'd rather stick a pencil in my eyeball than play sports with a bunch of skanky-assed cavemen."

A normal jock like Seth Sellers would kick my ass for saying that, sir. RC III just sort of giggled and hooted. Even though we never hung out after school or anything, we became buddies. He was always really happy to see me in the halls. I got him a summer job at Dante's Donuts too.

Yeah, I'm a good guy to know around here!

As I neared my house, I thought about what RC III

said, that I'm light on my feet. I used to be a swimmer (like Justin). I used to actually like gym.

I thought, *Maybe you can't ever get skinny, but you don't have to be a tub of turd either.* This thought repeated itself. *You've never been exactly skinny, but you weren't a tub of turd. Come on. Come on. No more tub of turd.* This thought gained some traction.

Before I walked into the front door of our dirty house, I sat down on the front step and breathed. Rita Day, our neighbor lady who used to do yoga with my mom, popped out of her garage. She gave me a big smile and a wave and then bounced around the side of the house with a garden bag. She's like sixty but jogs and is skinny and energetic to the point of being annoying. Grandpa's that way too. Energetic. Annoying.

I thought, *That's what I want.*

I thought, *Bouncy-ass six-pack muscle-head Grandpa.*

I pushed myself up off the step and went in.

"You want what now?" Grandpa asked when I found him in the kitchen.

"I want counseling," I said. "To not be like this, okay?" I pointed at my big self.

Grandpa fried eggs in a giant skillet. (Breakfast for

42

dinner is a big deal at my house.) "All you wanted last night was lasagna. You didn't want any salad," he said.

"I do now," I said.

"Too late," he said, pointing at the eggs.

"I want to get in shape. I want to get strong," I said.

"No, you don't," Grandpa said.

"Yes. Show me how to get strong," I said.

"It's not going to be easy," Grandpa said. "I don't believe you have it in you."

I looked down at the floor. "I don't want to be a turd anymore," I whispered.

Grandpa paused. I looked back up at him. He squinted, sizing me up. Steam and smoke poured off the eggs in front of him. The air crackled. "Did you steal money from me?" he asked. "I'm missing twenty bucks."

I paused. I swallowed. "Maybe," I said. I shut my eyes hard. "Yes."

"Uh-huh," he nodded. "Good to know."

I nodded back at him.

"Okay. We'll work you out tomorrow," he said. "Exercise. Start by eating only half the breakfast potatoes you normally do tonight. You overeat those carbohydrates, they turn to sugar, and you turn into a damn hippo with no energy. You got to stay in balance." He turned back to the stove and began flipping an egg.

"Well, why do you make that junk if it turns me into a fat ass?"

"Tuesday's veggie chili didn't go over too good, did it? Your dad told me never to make it again. He wants to suck crap as much as you do."

"Oh," I said. "Right."

Just then, Dad pulled into the garage.

"Don't tell Dad I'm doing this," I said.

"Why not? He could use some motivation," Grandpa said.

"Don't."

"Fine, fine." Grandpa nodded at me.

Sir, Justin Cornell called me Chunk. RC III said I should get in shape. He said I'm light on my feet.

After dinner, I texted Camille and Justin. I wrote, Need to speak immediately. We are definitely bamboozled. Go to Bitterroot for discussion?

Justin replied, I have some things I have to do tonight. Busy.

Camille replied, Playing poker with Grandma. Join us so we can discuss?

I wrote her back, Sounds really great, but no thanks. Talk tomorrow.

Camille always plays poker with her grandma. That wasn't a surprise. A month earlier, I would've been totally surprised by Justin being busy, but he'd begged off seeing me on weekends several times recently. I was suspicious but couldn't possibly have guessed what was really going on.

And so I went to bed at 8 p.m. This was how I went to war that first night. I moaned and dreamed about eating donuts because I was very, very, very hungry because I didn't eat much for dinner like Grandpa had said.

Early the next morning, I got donuts, just not in my mouth.

CHAPTER 6

Sir, I'm not lazy like that ass-pipe gym teacher Mr. McCartney would have you believe. In fact, I have no trouble getting up for work, okay? My first full summer day of work at Dante's Donuts began at 5:30 a.m.

I was up long before though. I sweated and then slept, dreamt about stuffing donuts in my face, then woke up and watched some crap on Netflix that just made me mad because it was stupid (something Justin recommended—*The Burps*). Then I slept. Then I was totally wide awake at 4:30. My brain ticked. My accounting brain (probably get it from Dad, who's the dean of accounting at MNLake Community College). It occurred to me that Kaus Company, owned by Kailey's dad, isn't the only food and drink company in town. Maybe another business might help the band out. Maybe my pal Dante of Dante's Donuts might add a nickel to his donut prices and donate the proceeds to the band. Couldn't that work? He's a Minnekota Lake band alum too. Couldn't we find a way around those Kaus jackasses?

Oh, yeah, I was getting mad at Kailey herself, even though I once loved her.

I thought, *Can't we raise our own cash and keep marching camp rolling?*

I needed to make some serious war plans.

I texted Justin and Camille what I believed about the band and the cheerleaders. Hear me right now! Cheer bitches took our money! Because it was before 5 a.m., neither responded.

Then I got ready for work.

When I left, Grandpa and Dad were sleeping in the living room. They'd been there all night—Grandpa snoring on the gross brown recliner, Dad sawing logs on the red couch Mom bought three months before she left us to be with a douche sack Mr. Mitsunori. (I'd like to punch his face.) A rerun of SportsCenter blared on the TV. This is the environment I'm growing up in, Mr. Rodriguez. It smelled like old man in the place.

No! You're not an old man, sir. You smell great!

Yeah, that's a little awkward.

Time to make the donuts. I walked out into dawn, fresh dew on the grass, new sun glowing in the trees. It's only a few blocks from my house to Main Street and Dante's old-timey, tourist-trap, brick-and-glass storefront. I walked with new purpose. *Gonna win!*

Dante usually has three kids there on the weekends during the summer, two or three during weekdays. Summers are busy as hell because of the resort traffic on the lake. As I mentioned, Dante had hired RC III. I got him to apply. Then Dante asked me what I thought of him. "RC III is one top-notch hombre," I said.

Dante did not, however, ask me about Chandra Gore. If he had, I would've been very, very negative on the matter.

Her eyes look like they're firing death at you! She wears black lipstick! She makes her cheeks look pale with makeup! Most of the time, she's wearing old, black lacy blouses like a dead old lady! Her fingernails are painted black! She wears skull rings and black boots! I'm a fan of her now, but really, that's not what I'd be looking for when hiring a cashier. Here's an interview question no businessman would ask: *Can you stare down customers and make them feel ice in their souls?*

But there she was. Gore was at Dante's before me. What a shock to my system! There's some really rough history surrounding Gore in my grade, and I just assumed Carrie Dragovich, who is one of Dad's students at the college, would be continuing to work at Dante's for the summer. But I walk in through the back door and there she is, the new hire, Gore herself sipping coffee out of a freaking Styrofoam cup.

I was all prepped to ask Dante to raise prices to support band, but I stopped sharp, wondered, *Is this some evil hallucination from not eating enough? Is she real?*

"Um…hi," Gore said. Her big ghost eyes popped out of her head. These were the first words I'd heard her say since seventh grade.

Isn't that weird, sir? Gore was in class with me every day. She was silent.

Then Dante came in from out front with his own cup of coffee. He wears a sailor's hat and white painter pants and a tight T-shirt all the time. Looks like he could be swabbing deck in the Navy. "Hey! Summertime!" he called to me.

"What is this?" I asked, pointing at Gore.

"This?" Dante asked.

"I'm a girl," Gore whispered.

"Summer help, buddy," Dante said.

"Where's Carrie?" I asked.

"Working on her dad's farm. You knew that," Dante said.

"No, this is not going to work," I said, again pointing at Gore. "She's a potential murderer."

Gore swallowed hard, then whispered, "You don't know anything." She turned and bolted for the bathroom. Even through her makeup, I could tell her skin was flushed.

"Unacceptable, dude. No good," Dante said. "You don't own this place. You don't treat my employees with disrespect. When Chandra is done with her business in there, you apologize to her or you go home. Understand?"

I bent toward Dante. I whispered, "She'll probably stab us before summer is through."

"I've known Chandra her whole life, Chunk. She's a sweet kid. Don't you go judging a book by its cover."

Well, Dante knew Chandra because her dad owns MNLake Bank. You know Darrell Wettlinger, right?

You gotta learn all these people's names if you're going to do business in this town, Mr. R.

51

The story?

Chandra threatened to kill people in middle school. Seriously. Three kids in my class—Kailey, Janessa, and Tyler Paul (who left town soon after, probably because his parents were freaked). She also threatened Seth Sellers, a grade ahead of us. (I approved of that.) She wrote them notes saying she'd cut their throats in the middle of the night and that they'd better watch out. It was a big deal. She was suspended. Her dad had to petition the school board to get her back in. I was friends with all those guys in seventh grade (except Seth). They were so scared.

Of course, they'd all been psychotically mean to her before she made death threats.

Yeah. Things were bad for her.

In any case, RC III showed up before Gore even got out of the bathroom. I trained him. Dante trained her. Gore didn't look at me for the rest of the morning. Not even when I apologized.

"Sorry," I said.

"Okay," she whispered, staring above my head. She's almost six feet tall, so it's easy for her to stare over my head.

Yeah. I did feel bad about going off half-cocked like

that. A little. Mostly, I felt like jamming every damn donut in the store in my damn mouth because I was so damn hungry!

I didn't stuff anything though. Grandpa was planning a workout for me after donuts. I didn't want to barf all over his old fart shoes.

RC III did well. Gore did too. They learned the donut-selling business fast.

With the new employee training, I didn't get a chance to ask Dante about helping the band until nearly closing time at 2 p.m., when everybody was cleaning up (Gore out front sweeping). "Hey, Dante, would you add a nickel to your donuts and donate to the band?" I asked.

RC III looked up from washing a rack.

Dante said, "What now?" He stood holding this big metal spoon (sort of looked like he was going to whack me with it).

I swallowed, strained my brain, and said something like, "Donuts. Lost our funding. Help the band?" I wasn't articulate. My leadership bone was so weak, Mr. R.

"What the hell?" he asked again.

"Pop machine funding. Dance squad took our money. No summer band. School-sanctioned theft."

Dante turned a little red. "No way," he said.

"Totally," I said.

"Really?" RC III asked.

"Really," I said. "We need money or else—"

Dante shook his head and winced. "Jesus. I can't change my prices. I'd have to redo all my signs and printed materials. That's costly."

"Oh," I said. "Hm."

"I've got no budget for that."

"Right," I said.

Then he took a deep breath and said, "How about you come up with a bake sale or a special event that maybe I can sponsor?"

"Hm," I said. "Yeah?"

"Something not stupid, Chunk," he said. "Propose an event and we'll see. Maybe."

Sure. That was a start, I guess.

No, Justin never responded to my early morning text calling out the cheer bitches. Camille did though. We agreed to get together after my workout at 5 p.m.

"Workout?" she asked.

That's right. Workout.

CHAPTER 7

Project Kill Chunk. Why do you want to hear about this?

Yeah, I'm a real motivational figure, sir. Big time.

Okay. First, to picture this adequately, you must know that my grandpa has no shame with regard to his body. Even though he's an old man, he walks around the yard in compaction shorts and nothing else. He should be in Under Armour advertising for old farts. Got that visualized in your mind?

It shouldn't be surprising that he has no fear of nakedness. He spent his youth wearing a banana hammock, making his oiled-up pecs bulge for crowds of people. That would help a guy feel comfortable being half-naked in the hood.

These days, he's into fitness, not bodybuilding. He built a fitness room next to my room in the basement (the laundry room). He hung a bunch of motivational posters on the wall and brought down a bunch of medicine balls and a couple yoga balls and those kettlebell weights that Russian wrestlers use.

I'd never touched any of it. When Grandpa works out, I go upstairs. His grunting and sweating are pretty distracting. The laundry room will never smell the same—I'll tell you that.

Grandpa wore his compaction shorts with a tucked-in tank top. He wore wristbands and a sweatband on his crew cut head. He was barefoot (no old man shoes for me to barf on).

I wore my XL Dante's Donuts T-shirt, which is the tightest shirt I'll wear, and a pair of elastic waistband khakis because the stretchies don't pinch my loaf, if you know what I mean.

"You have anything more comfortable?" Grandpa asked.

"No," I said.

"Sweats?" he asked.

"No," I said.

"We have to do something about your clothes. That shirt will restrict you. Take it off."

"No," I said. "I can't do that. Are you kidding me?"

"Why would I be kidding?" he asked.

"No," I said.

He shrugged. "Suit yourself."

He set up stations—burpees, push-ups, mountain climbers, yoga ball crunches, medicine ball squats, and medicine ball military presses. He showed me how to do each. (I'd done all this crap in gym at some point in my long academic career.) Then he put me on the clock, "Thirty seconds for each exercise. Thirty seconds rest between exercises. We'll go around the circuit three times. Eighteen minutes of hell," he said.

"Great," I said (sarcastic).

"You asked for this."

"Great," I said.

Then he shouted, "Go, Chunk! Burpees first. Let's do it!"

I started with burpees (squatting and then kicking back into a push-up position, then crunching up and standing). After a few, I cried, "Almost done?"

"Fifteen seconds," he said. "Go!"

I tried to go. I wanted to go, but my body did not go. Lightning fired in my shoulders. The back of my neck cramped up. At the end of thirty seconds, I thought I might puke. Sweat poured from me. I sucked for air. The basement floor spun beneath me.

"Good work!" Grandpa shouted. And then he cried, "Push-ups!"

By push-up four, I was down on my knees. Grandpa shouted above me, but it didn't matter. "Do girl push-ups!" he cried, but I couldn't. I spent fifteen of the thirty seconds with my face pressed to the gross basement floor.

It went like this with mountain climbers too. Ten seconds of go. Twenty seconds of heaving for air on the floor while Grandpa screamed above me. Yoga ball crunches turned into a crunch or two and then me draped upside down over a yoga ball while Grandpa shouted. Squats became little dips. Then finally there were military presses, which meant lifting a heavy object above my head over and over.

You can't slack off with a ball over your head. You can't lie down or lie back. You do it or you don't. I did it five or six times, my neck charley-horsing, backs of my arms trembling. Then I moved to *don't* because I couldn't.

"Push it up, Chunky! Push it up!" Grandpa shouted.

As I struggled to lift that damn ball, Grandpa

slapped my hips hard. I cried out in pain and my fat rippled and waved. Grandpa shouted, "Go on, chub!" He slapped my hips again and I slammed the ball onto the floor in front of me.

"Bullshit!" he shouted.

"Stick it in your ass!" I shouted back.

He glared, his jaw clenched, the whistle on his phone blew, and he dropped down onto the concrete floor and reeled off like thirty push-ups. I stood there sweating and dizzy while he did it, breathing hard, staring at that ball I'd slammed on the floor, thinking about grabbing it and crushing Grandpa in the head. Before I could, he popped back up and put his mug right in my face. He said, "That's what you do with your anger, Chunky. You squeeze out the pain and pump out the reps. You get it?"

"No," I said.

"Then you'll die a fat ass."

"So," I said.

"So don't ask for help, fat ass."

I yanked the effenheimer out on him, then ran and locked myself in the bathroom.

I sat on the toilet. My gut bulged out between my legs. I held my head in my hands.

Grandpa knocked, came in. He just said, "Shower up, son. You did good, okay? Pain is good. Pain is gain. That was a good start. We'll get her even better tomorrow."

I probably stayed in the bathroom for two hours.

Around four o'clock, Grandpa made me a salad. He put some boiled chicken in there so I didn't actually die of hunger.

That was very, very hard. Workout and boiled chicken—both.

Things were about to get harder.

CHAPTER 8

Dad got home from teaching his Saturday class at 4:45. "Boiled chicken?" he asked.

"That's what we have. Take it or leave it," Grandpa said.

Dad grumbled. "You ate this?" he asked me.

"Uh," I said. I didn't say *uh* because I was against the chicken. I said *uh* because I had no energy. My flesh had gone all trembly and weak. The eighteen minutes of hell workout (or ten minutes or whatever it had actually been) destroyed me. Muscles in my legs twitched. My back spasmed. My head swam. Scared me, sir. I wondered if I was having a stroke.

I pulled on my shoes though. I got ready to go.

At 5 p.m., right on time, Camille rolled up in her dad's pickup truck.

I left the house and climbed in. "Cornell coming?" I asked.

"He didn't answer my texts," she said.

"He didn't reply to me this morning either," I said.

"He wouldn't answer my calls last night. He texted about how he's been tired lately," she said.

"Huh. That's truly weird," I said.

"Chunk," Camille said.

"What?"

"Has he mentioned anything to you?"

"No. About what?" I asked.

"About maybe not liking me?" Camille asked.

"Oh, no. Uh-uh," I said. But that wasn't exactly the truth.

Camille has crushed on Justin for a couple years and he asked me in April why she never got a real haircut and why she wore her pants so high. (I didn't know what he meant even—except she has these blue thrift shop hippie bell bottoms that make her look like she's in 1970.) "Camille is pretty cute, right?" Justin had said.

"Yeah. Definitely," I replied.

"But she's just too weird," he said. "I wish she'd wear normal clothes, man."

He and Camille went to prom together, even

though he wasn't enthusiastic about it, even though a year earlier all he talked about was how great it was going to be when he finally got up the courage to make a move on her.

Yeah, he liked her before! Forever! Until the last month or whatever.

Here's the sad truth, Mr. Rodriguez. Over the past year, Justin's grown from a pencil-neck geek to looking sort of like Clark Kent. He's on the swim team and he grew all these muscles out of no place. The last time we hung out just the two of us, maybe three weeks ago, he said the weirdest thing while we were eating this thick and chewy chocolate cake his mom had made.

My memories always revolve around food. I love his mom by the way.

He said, "Chicks dig me."

Chicks *dig* me! What the hell, right? I asked him how he gained this saintly knowledge and he was pretty nonspecific on the matter, except to say he had been catching a little buzz on the Interweb. *What?!*

He did get multiple texts that night and he wouldn't tell me who they were from, which is ridiculous because we were buddies. I went on family vacations with him!

I stayed overnight at his house like a thousand times! His dad loves me, calls me *Coolio*! His mom makes me cakes and pies because my mom left me! Then out of the blue, he won't tell me who he's texting with? That hurts, man. Seriously.

"No," I said to Camille. "He hasn't mentioned anything."

"Something has gone wrong," Camille said.

"I…I don't know," I said.

Camille took a deep breath and then shouted, "Screw Justin Cornell!"

I didn't say *In your dreams*, which was on the tip of my dumb tongue.

"Now what about these bamboozling cheer bitches?" Camille asked.

I told her my hunch and it was really just a hunch at that time. Firstly, all funding for marching camp comes from the pop machine. Secondly, Shaver loves summer marching camp and wouldn't cancel it unless suddenly the money to do it was gone. And thirdly, why cheerleaders? The same week the pop price goes up, the new dance squad is announced and marching is suddenly canceled? These are not disconnected events.

Camille pulled the pickup truck over. She said, "I don't believe you."

I said, "I know in my heart I'm right."

She said, "I need to talk to Shaver."

I was like, "What?"

Camille swung the pickup around, nearly creaming a kid on a bike. She headed toward Shaver's shit-ball condo right off Main Street.

"We're going to a teacher's house?"

"He needs to verify the situation," Camille said. "Otherwise, I refuse to believe it."

A few minutes later, we pulled up in front of Shaver's place. He and Mrs. Shaver got divorced last year. He moved from Lion's Ridge by Kailey to that hole, poor guy.

Even though it was a nice evening, his shades were all pulled down. "Doesn't look home," I said. Then we got out of the car and heard Led Zeppelin muffled but clearly vibrating through his walls.

"He's home," Camille said. "He's rocking out."

"I don't like it," I said.

Camille marched right up to his front door and rang the bell. His walls were literally shaking to that *hey hey mama* song.

He didn't answer.

"Maybe the bell doesn't work?" Camille said.

"Maybe he can't hear it?" I said.

Camille pounded on the door. We waited. The song got to that *ah ah ah* part, which is a little quieter, and Camille pounded again. Then the song took off and we stood there. Then Camille said, "I'm going in."

"No!"

She nodded and twisted the doorknob and the door was open. And Camille walked right in! Balls, man! She left the door open behind her and I didn't know what to do, so I followed.

Adrenaline gave me a little strength. At least I wasn't bodily trembling from my ten minutes of hell (and lack of Dew and lack of normal, satisfying, but deadly food).

Shaver was right on the other side of the door, sitting in his living room on the couch, wearing these colorful plaid shorts and nothing else. He had an ashtray and this bottle of whiskey balanced on his big bare gut. Dude was sucking right from the bottle. Lit cigarette in the other hand.

My eyes burned. I thought of Shaver in his prime, teaching us new parts for a new piece, big smile on his face, conducting, gesturing small to make us quiet, gesturing huge to make us loud. Waving his arms around crying, "Let's hear it! Let's hear it!" He's such a good teacher, but there he was shirtless with whiskey.

Camille walked over to his stereo (old school) and turned down the volume.

"Hey, brother," he nodded at me. "Hey, girl," he smiled at Camille.

"You're loaded," Camille said.

"You're breaking and entering," Shaver smiled.

"You're a teacher!" Camille said.

The smile left his face. "Maybe. Maybe not," Shaver said. "Maybe not." He shook his head and shut his eyes. "Maybe?" He opened his eyes and swigged on the whiskey and then puffed his cigarette.

"God," Camille said. She looked at me. I shrugged. "Mr. Shaver," she said.

"Yes, ma'am?"

"Chunk says the cheerleaders took the pop money and that's why camp was canceled."

"Oh?" Mr. Shaver asked.

"Is it true?"

"Is it?" he asked back.

"I believe it's true," I said.

"Chunk would know," Shaver said to Camille. "Boy has hidden powers of deep wisdom and knowledge." Then he laughed, which I didn't appreciate.

"So it's true?" Camille said. "If it's true, then we've been bamboozled."

Again, the smile left Shaver's face. He grunted. He sat forward and the ashtray slid down his gut and spilled. He plunked the whiskey bottle onto the side table. "You, girl." He pointed at Camille. "Don't make trouble for me."

"What?"

He shook his head. He said, "I'm asking you man-to-man. No trouble."

"She's not a man," I said.

"Then I'm asking you."

"Chunk isn't a man either," Camille said.

"This isn't your business," Shaver said.

"Oh, my God. It's true," Camille said. "How could they do that? How could they just take our money?"

Shaver's face went slack. He leaned back in the chair. "Kaus is a lady from hell," he said.

"What?" Camille asked.

"Please leave."

"You said Kaus!" I shouted.

"You try standing up to that school board."

"You have to stand up," Camille said.

"No."

"Can we raise the money?" I asked. "For the camp?"

"Good luck to you," Shaver said.

"Don't be a wimp!" Camille shouted. "You have to stand up!"

"Time for you to leave, Ms. Buzzkill. Right now," Shaver said. "I'll call the cops."

"We are *gone*," Camille hissed.

She blew out the door. I followed behind her. We climbed in her truck. Camille pulled out fast.

"See?" I said. "Told you."

"Oh, my God. We have to do something. We have to raise money and get our camp back," Camille said. "For Shaver and for us."

"For Shaver?"

"He's losing it. Did you see…He used to be so… so—"

"Great."

"Yeah." Camille blinked.

She took a left and pulled around by the lake. We drove past the Wilson Beach parking lot. There was a silver Honda Civic in the lot. Justin's car, I'm sure. Luckily, Camille didn't see it.

"Listen. I already talked to Dante. He'll sponsor us if we have a bake sale or something, an event of some kind."

"Really?" Camille asked. "You did something?"

"Why is that surprising?"

"We need something big, Chunk. We need it fast. Camp is in a week. Would Dante give us a lot of money?"

"No," I said. "Definitely not. He'll give us some donuts."

"Uh-huh," Camille said. She drove way too slow through town. Cars honked at us, but she didn't pay any attention. "We need to make a big event."

"A very big event," I said and nodded. "Huge."

"Like a dance or a…a bachelor auction or art auction or we could go door-to-door and sell donuts?" Camille said.

"We are a band," I said. "How about a concert?"

"Oh, that's…that's pretty good," Camille said,

nodding. She pulled the truck over to the side of the road. Some dude in a Pontiac shouted at us, I assume about how slow we were going. Camille took in a deep breath and nodded more. "Yeah. Totally. We're a band and we can play our instruments!"

We stared at each other with our mouths hanging open like fools, sir, like we'd just heard a message from God. Then we tried to high-five but totally missed. People like Camille should never high-five.

I can high-five. I'm good like that. With the right person.

It wasn't a great idea really. We had no time to organize the thing. Camille became obsessed with this concert though. She stayed obsessed with it even after it was way too late.

I don't know, sir. I guess I let Camille take charge at first because my leadership bone was in poor condition. I really didn't think anyone would listen to me anyway.

When she dropped me off at home, she said, "I'll come up with a poster for the concert!"

"Uh-huh," I said. "Great." I'd already begun thinking of all the problems and our lack of time. I couldn't see how we'd do it without Justin either. Justin is so good at organizing stuff.

Inside, I texted him, What are you doing? Where are you? Need your help on this. Camille organizing concert. Me too.

He wrote back, At Wilson Beach with Sellers, Emily, and Janessa. Come down?

It was a hard slap in the face. I blinked. My eyes watered. I almost fell over, sir. Seth Sellers, Emily Yu, and Janessa Rogers? I stared at that text. My heart beat hard in my chest. My mouth got dry. *Janessa?*

It just didn't seem possible. I read and reread the text. Then I got mad.

I didn't want Justin to show Seth, Emily, and Janessa a crazy upset text from a psycho blimp. (Janessa sometimes called me a psycho blimp.) So I didn't send one until later. Even though I worked early in the morning, I stayed up until 1 a.m., burning up, man. Then I thumbed the shit in.

Way to drop your friends at first sign of popularity, man. Rude to Camille? Hanging with douche Janessa and Sellers? Don't give a shit that band got screwed? Good going!

About ten minutes later, a text came back. 1. Janessa is my girlfriend. I wanted to tell you about what was going on last week, but you were flipping out. Please don't call her names ever again. 2. Stop being a drama queen. It's band camp, not the Holocaust. Talk tomorrow.

Oh, man, sir. Oh, crap. This can't be real. This is a joke. I tried to thumb up a response, but I couldn't do it. Janessa Rogers. Eventually, I threw my phone on the floor.

Yeah, that's right. Mystery texts? Buzz on the Interweb? Justin "Clark Kent" Cornell, my dork friend, scored the biggest shit-face girl ever to exist in our grade.

She's like a beach volleyball player on TV. What do you think he finds interesting about her? She wears tight pants and she looks super fine. She's part of Minnekota Lake's evil Charlie's Angels (with Kailey and Emily). Justin likes to win. He wins at every-thing. Debate. Swim team. Hot girls. He certainly isn't hanging with Janessa Rogers because she's sweet and wonderful because she's the exact opposite. She's terrible and mean. But she's hot and she doesn't dress weird like Camille.

Makes me sick.

Seriously terrible.

Screw it.

Just screw it.

Do we get lunch, Mr. Rodriguez? I haven't eaten anything since yesterday.

Gross. I'll take the salad.

CHAPTER 9

Yeah, I like the ham part. Cubed ham. Pretty delicious. I like the cheese part and the ranch dressing part too. But the lettuce—

I will choke down the lettuce because I need roughage. Roughage for health. That's what Grandpa says. He has to have half his calories in roughage or he can't take a dump. Disgusting, dude. Like that's what I want to think about while I'm eating dinner. Grandpa's ability to take a crap.

It's better with him here than when it was just Dad and me. That was pretty bad. We were dying in the swamp of despair. Dad went to work. I went to school. We got home, ordered pizza, watched TV until we passed out. I'd wake up with my guts burning at like 3 a.m. and go to bed. At school, I couldn't concentrate because I was so tired. Last half of eighth grade, I slept a lot in class. (Code Red stopped that in high school.)

And I got pulled out of the top math group and reading group and I quit swimming and track. (I always sucked anyway—I mean, I liked it, but whatever.) I could only stay awake for band, it seemed like (my savior, band). And Dad never went to bed. He slept on this broken-down recliner for like two years.

He didn't want to sleep in Mom's bed. She picked it out. Giant, king-sized, space-aged foam. Mom bought that bed as part of her freaking-out spending binge, which left us seriously broke.

Yeah. Her online boyfriend's friend showed up in Minnekota on this Saturday morning right before Christmas. The lady took Mom to the airport in the Cities and then Mom went to Japan. Mom had been crying and stuffing crap in a big suitcase for like an hour and Dad was shouting at her. And I stood there in the door—I mean, I had just turned fourteen, sir. I didn't know what the hell was going on. Right before she left, she put her hands on my cheeks, swallowed really hard, and said, "Take care of your father, okay?" She was totally bawling at that point.

I have no idea how she hooked up with a Japanese architect. It's a weird mystery. Sort of. I mean, not that big a mystery. Mom turned into a Zen Buddhist a few years ago and she did yoga and bought all these plants that she snipped at with scissors. And she refused to eat anything but rice and she got a tattoo of some Japanese character on her shoulder. She lost about a million pounds (got down to like a hundred) and then she started closing herself in her office at night while Dad and I watched TV. I'm sure she was Skyping that Mitsunori.

I really don't know how they met in the first place.

Of course, I still like her. She's my mom. I love her because I have to. I just do because I miss her. She used to be really funny and noisy. Dad is the opposite of funny. Her laugh sounded like a goose honk.

Canada goose. The house was noisy until she got Zen.

When I was little, we were alone a lot because Dad was getting his PhD at St. Thomas, so he lived in the Cities part time. I thought it was pretty great. She *was* great. A nice mom. We went to the playground all the time with Kailey and her mom. Even in the winter, we did a bunch of stuff outside. Ice-skating on the lake. She just got excited about fresh air, you know? The fresh air was good for me. I was normal back then at least. I didn't have to buy stretchy pants because regular kid pants fit just fine. Took a couple of years of Dad being around full time (moved up to head of accounting at the school) for Mom to get fat and tired and stupid and sad like the rest of us.

Then she got Zen and she stopped honking like a goose and got skinny. And she got a Japanese boyfriend, who she probably talked to on her computer all night. Good times. Ha-ha.

She doesn't even email me, sir. It's like I no longer exist at all.

Hey. Let me eat my stupid roughage, okay?

CHAPTER 10

Okay. I guess it seemed reasonable. Spunk River Days. June 14, 15, and 16, right? Right there on Wilson Beach. Bunch of rock bands (including Wall of Sound from Minneapolis, which features an MLAHS band alum, which would've been a good tie-in to our fund-raising), softball tournament, a few measly rides run by dudes with no teeth, a bunch of carnival games, and cotton candy and slushies and crap. A tractor pull. Usually lots of bees and mosquitoes too. Takes place before band camp was supposed to start the following week (tomorrow). Seemed like the right time and place to do a fund-raiser for the band. I agreed with Camille on that point.

Well, there were other points that should've been addressed before Camille started spreading the word, like where would we have this concert if the Wilson Beach band shell has already been booked for a year?

How would we get word out to the town? How would we actually make any money? Pass a hat or charge admission and how do you charge admission if you're outside? Also, how would we practice? What songs? Who would actually show up to blow their horns? Who would direct if Mr. Shaver drowned himself in booze and cigarettes and then took off in his car?

Camille came into Dante's around ten o'clock the next morning. She walked in and stopped in her tracks. She and Gore stared at each other. I had failed to mention to Camille the night before that Gore was now my coworker.

"What are you looking at?" Gore asked.

Gore scares people, sir. Some people. What's weird is she's great at the counter. Really chatty and nice. Customers from the Twin Cities clearly like her because they don't understand her history. Camille knows though, so she was scared.

Camille looked over at me. I shrugged. Then she held up a flier for the concert.

"Nice butterfly," Gore said.

"Thanks?" Camille responded.

Gore was right. Nice butterfly. Camille had drawn

a sweet-looking butterfly floating over the shore of Minnekota Lake. She'd written underneath it, "MLAHS Marching Band Spunk River Fund-raiser!" She'd written, "Sponsored by Dante's Donuts." She had a slot for date, time, place, and price but hadn't filled any of that in.

"What do you think?" she asked.

"Pretty good!" I said.

"It's stupid," she said.

"Why?" I asked.

"I'm a child," she said.

"What?" I didn't get it, sir. It was a nice butterfly.

"I'm just drawing pictures like a little kid, not getting anything done. I mean, where are we going to play?" she asked.

"And when?" I asked.

"Why?" Gore asked, as if she were a part of the conversation.

"Why what?" Camille asked.

"Why are you having a fund-raiser for the band?" Gore asked.

"Cheerleaders are using all the money from the pop machine," Camille said.

"What?" Gore whispered. "What?" she said again.

"Cheerleaders?" Camille said.

"I heard you," Gore whispered. Then she spoke so quietly Camille and I had to lean in to hear. "That's false advertising for consumers, you know? Because I only bought pop out of that machine because the sign said it went to the band. I wouldn't have given those girls my money. Not for any reason. I'm very angry about this."

"I'm sorry?" Camille said.

"It's not your fault," Gore whispered.

Dante came out from in back. He nodded at Camille. He pointed at Gore and me and said, "Get ready for the church rush, you two." Then he looked at the flier in Camille's hand. He blinked. He turned a little red. "I'm sponsoring what?" he said.

"Spunk River Band Fund-raiser?" Camille said.

"Chunk," Dante said, "I'd like a word." He turned and stomped into the back.

"Why'd you put that on the poster?" I whispered to Camille.

"But you said...I don't know—It's just a draft!"

"You are just playing. You are a little kid," I hissed.

I turned and walked in back.

Dante gave me the business. Squawked at me about pulling the wool over his eyes and crap like that. I calmed him down, told him it was just a draft. Dante's a little explosive, I've figured out. Drama queen, right?

No. We're cool. We're pals.

What wasn't cool is I totally offended Camille by calling her a kid. She's so damn sensitive. When I came back out from talking to Dante, she was gone.

"You made your girlfriend cry," Gore whispered.

"She's not my girlfriend."

"Oh," Gore said.

"Crap," I said.

Poor Camille didn't even know the Janessa/Justin news and there I was insulting her, you know? Felt bad.

"Can I help?" Gore asked.

"With what?"

"Plan your concert so I can *not* get too mad about spending all my lemonade money on girls who have made my life a living hell forever," Gore said.

"Oh. Well. I. Hm. Maybe?"

Oh, that's just what we need, the murderer helping out. That will attract the crowds!

"Okay," Gore said. She smiled at me. She has a pretty smile. She's not an odd outsider sad sack because she's hard on the eyes. She's a sad sack because she threatened to murder kids.

After my shift, I texted Camille that I was sorry. She texted, Whatever. Sorry!!!!!

Call me later, she wrote.

This is your first summer in town, right, Mr. Rodriguez?

Yeah, Spunk River Days is one sick name, but that's the river that goes into Minnekota Lake, so what are you going to do? All the high school kids make disgusting jokes about Spunk River Days.

I'm sure you can imagine what they say.

Always cracks me up when I think about a pioneer coming across the little river and saying, "We shall call this waterway Spunk!"

CHAPTER 11

Grandpa and I jumped rope for a half hour in the afternoon. I was so sore from the day before, but I didn't cry.

That's progress. Go team!

Not pretty. I was downstairs lying on the floor of my room, scribbling some dumb poetry about food into my ideas notebook. (*I would kill for a soft bed of bread and a slice of ham spread across me.* Crap like that.) I was listening to music, so I didn't even hear her ring the doorbell or Grandpa let her in.

I was shirtless. Camille came down the stairs and walked around the corner into my bedroom and I jumped, hit my head on the underside of my bed (a foldout couch), and then tried to roll under it so she wouldn't see me. I got lodged under there pretty good. I haven't had my shirt off in front of the opposite sex, you know...since Mom and the poundage. I sure didn't want anyone seeing my business, okay?

And no girl had ever been in my room! (I mean, other than Mom.) (Oh…and Doris.)

It's pretty gross. The room was a rec room for the family that built the place in the 70s. When Mom decided she needed an office a few years ago (probably for illicit Skyping purposes), down I went. It's this shiny wood paneling and some rugs on the tile floor and this old foldout couch. (My bed was too small, so we didn't move it. It was a little boy bed.) Other than the wood, the walls are pretty bare, except a poster of Grandpa in his bodybuilding prime (which I realize is a little weird because he's pretty much naked) and a picture of me that Dad took while I played a trombone solo at the spring jazz concert. Me and my naked Grandpa. My room doesn't exactly flatter, you know?

I don't know how she reacted. I was under the bed!

"What are you doing, Gabe?" Camille asked.

"Looking for…a sock. Socks. You scared me."

"Do you need help?" she asked.

"No. Could you leave for a second? I'm not decent, okay?"

"Yeah. Sure. Sorry. I should've knocked. I didn't even think to—"

"Just go," I shouted from under the bed. A spring was digging into my shoulder pretty bad.

Camille disappeared into the laundry room and I unglued my body from under the bed (big bump on my head and a scratch on my shoulder blade). I pulled on my giant Nirvana T-shirt and tried to shake out the cobwebs in my brain. I'd made it through two days of not eating donuts at work, but I'll tell you this—donuts didn't just disappear. They were on my mind. Like *in* my mind. So were sandwiches. Lots of them. Lodged in my head. I just kept thinking about the sweet relief of eating filled donuts or sipping down some pop. That's why I wrote the poetry.

Diet is not pop. Diet tastes like rat poison, so no, I didn't drink any of that.

I called Camille back in and she was weird. At first, I thought it was because she'd seen my semi-naked body and that had grossed her out, which made me feel bad. But it soon became evident that she'd talked to Justin.

Because I didn't want her in my room, we climbed

the stairs and went out to the patio in the backyard. Grandpa eyeballed us as we passed. He knew I had a friend that was a girl, but Camille hadn't ever spent time at the house since he'd been there. He nodded at me and winked.

No, there's nothing between me and Camille Gardener. Don't ask again.

After we sat down, Camille took in a deep breath and said, "Justin isn't going to participate."

"In what?" I asked.

"The concert."

I shook my head. (I mean, I already sort of knew he wouldn't do it.) "Wow. Are you kidding?" Actually, Justin was one of the big problems with the concert I'd already begun to consider. He's first chair trumpet. He wins trumpet like he wins everything. Trumpets are important to a band. We'd sound like crap without him. "Why?" I asked. (I knew why.)

"He says he doesn't have the time."

"But he barely works."

"He doesn't work. He doesn't start teaching swim lessons until June 24," Camille cried.

I mean, she cried, sir. As in crying.

"Did he tell you?" I asked.

"Tell me what? That he broke up with me? That he has someone new?"

Oh, man. Dating? Crazy Camille. "You guys were dating?" I asked. "I didn't know."

"Weren't we?" Camille asked. "What does dating mean? We went to movies and prom and out for coffee and we did homework together. Isn't that dating?"

"Other than prom, I was with you for all of that."

"We weren't dating?" Camille shouted.

I mean, she shouted, sir. Seriously.

"I don't know," I said, shrugging. "I mean, if you two were dating, then I was dating you too, right?"

"Who is she?" Camille shouted. "Who is he dating?"

"Oh? Who?" I asked. I figured Justin had confessed about Janessa.

"Is there someone else?" she cried.

Grandpa came out and said, "You're waking the dead. Keep it down."

"Sorry," Camille said.

He grumbled something and eyeballed me in a way that said *Get rid of the psycho hippie* and then he shut himself back inside.

No, I couldn't tell her, Mr. Rodriguez. It was at the tip of my tongue, you know? I wanted to get the news out there into the world because I was pretty upset about it too. But I couldn't say the words, "Justin Cornell is dating Janessa Rogers." Especially not with Camille so crazy and loud already.

What did I say? Something like, "He'll rue the day, Camille. He'll be sorry about all this." Judging from last night, I think he does rue the day. Maybe.

"We can do this without him," Camille whispered. "You and me."

Before she took off, we posted to the band's Facebook page.

Something like, MLAHS Peppers and Marchers, would you like to participate in a Spunk River Days fund-raising concert? Let's raise money and save marching camp!

In an hour, there were about thirty comments. They all said something like, Money? Why money? Whose money? What money? Is this money for you, Camille? (Camille did the post.) Austin Bates, who's this 90s gangster rapper wannabe, posted, Y'all are stupid bitches.

We seriously failed to communicate the money situation, sir. I did. It was my job because I was the one who had figured out that something had gone amiss, right?

Yeah, Shaver knew too. He should've been doing something. Last year, when the school board tried to get rid of the fall play, Ms. Feagan organized a letter-writing campaign. The *Minnekota Lake Journal* was filled with letters of support for the drama program. And when the school board met, like three hundred people showed up and it didn't go through. Fall play is going strong. Ms. Feagan is meritorious, as I've said.

No, I don't believe there were public meetings. Not real ones. I've looked back through weeks of newspapers and there weren't any postings about upcoming school board meetings. All the crap that went down about the band was hidden.

That's illegal, right?

No, Shaver sure didn't handle this stuff very well, maybe because he, like Dad, couldn't handle the breakup of his own family?

That's just guessing. I'm trying to figure out why Shaver, a totally great teacher, shot out into the outer limits like he did.

At like two in the morning, in response to Camille's Facebook concert thing, he posted, Don't you bother!

I'm assuming Shaver made that post before his arrest. You should ask the cops what time they pulled him over. Teachers getting drunk-driving tickets? That's not good. Maybe a teacher could fly under the radar up in the Cities. But in Minnekota, you get your butt pulled over for being a dangerous idiot and the whole town knows about it within a few hours. On the radio, in the paper, bubbling out of every convenience store clerk's piehole, right?

That's probably just what's happening to me right now. Everybody chattering about the fat boy breaking and entering. Glad I'm locked in here instead of being out there in the cruel world.

RC III and Gore were scheduled at Dante's for the morning, so I wasn't in. In fact, I was sleeping like a big gourd in the garden when my phone buzzed.

Gore had heard first thing because Dante rocks out to the local station and they were broadcasting it every ten minutes. *Minnekota Lake Area High School band teacher Barry Shaver was arrested this morning for driving under the influence.* She doesn't carry a cell, which is weird, but she's weird. She called from the store's number.

When I saw it was from Dante's, I freaked a little. Answered, "Oh, crap, am I supposed to be in?"

"Gabe?" a very quiet girl voice said.

"Who is this?" I asked.

"You're not supposed to be at work."

"Good. Who is this?"

"Chandra Wettlinger," Gore said.

"Why are you calling me?" I demanded. I blinked. My eyes burned from sleep.

"Your band teacher was arrested. I thought you'd want to know. The news keeps playing on the radio."

"Oh, man." It felt like a hot poker pierced my chest. "Oh, crap." I couldn't breathe. "Is he okay?"

"I think so. I don't know. He might have a bad headache," Gore whispered.

"Did he get in a fight or something?"

"Driving drunk," Gore said.

"Oh, no."

"Yeah, it's not good news," Gore whispered. "I'd better get to the counter. It's busy."

We paused, both of us.

"Hello?" she said.

"Thanks for calling, Gore," I said.

Then she sort of laughed. "I don't think you're supposed to call me that to my face."

"Sorry."

"Bye, Gabe," she said.

What an idiot, huh? Turns out Gore likes the nickname Gore. But really, that's just a stroke of luck. It's like if she got off the phone by saying, "Thanks for calling, lard ass." How would I feel about that? I'm as bad as the rest, man.

I used to be anyway.

Even though it was only like seven in the morning, I texted Camille. She'd just heard. She called back instead of texting, which I normally wouldn't appreciate, as I don't really like talking on the phone. But this was pretty huge. "Did you see what Shaver posted to Facebook?" she asked.

"No," I replied. "I'm just getting up."

"Check it out. I'm beginning to worry we're going to lose band completely. What if they fire him?"

"Lose band?" I whispered.

"Shaver's a criminal now," Camille said.

"I can't lose band!" I shouted.

"What's with all the shouting?" Grandpa shouted from upstairs.

I pulled the phone from my ear. "Shut up," I shouted at him.

"What's going on?" Camille shouted from the phone.

I put the phone back to my ear. "I have to go," I said to Camille.

Here's the deal, Mr. Rodriguez. Band has been my life, right? I mean, Jesus. Who would I even be? Nobody. My horn playing is the only consistent claim to any kind of excellence and love I've got. I really don't do anything else.

"No," I whispered. "No—"

On Friday, I'd made this declaration of war, but I didn't really know what I was fighting for. I was just super pissed. Down there in the basement at that moment, I realized I was fighting for my life.

I opened up my laptop and got on the band's Facebook page. I read through the comments, including Shaver's early morning Don't you bother! I became enraged. These lazy bandmate jerks were giving

Camille lip? Giving me lip? (No, they didn't know I was with her when she posted—but still.) Mr. Shaver said not to bother? Were we the only ones who cared? I got jacked up as hell and then I wrote. I figured everyone would just make crap of me, but I didn't care.

Go ahead, sir, pull up the post. It's public.

Gabe Johnson, June 10 at 7:25 a.m. near Minnekota, MN.

You fools, listen up. First, we are all seriously fools! Why? Because second, the cheer squad dance team— or whatever the hell they are—has been given all the money from the pop machine. I don't know who did this, but I assume it's Deevers and the Kaus family. We don't have marching band because the school district is clearly, silently taking potshots at our program. Now our idiot teacher is getting arrested. (Oh, don't you bother, Shaver, you jerk!) That plays right into their hands, okay? They could easily get rid of Shaver altogether and take the band from us. Who needs music at the basketball games and football games if there's a bunch of girls in skirts jumping around? Get your heads out of your asses. If you care about band at MLAHS at all, you'd better message me today. Got it? You freaking Geekers are pissing me off.

I slammed my computer shut and screamed up at Grandpa, "Is Dad home?"

"More shouting, huh?" he shouted.

"Is Dad home?" I shouted again.

"Left for work."

"Let's work out right now!"

A couple minutes later, Grandpa came down the stairs in his compaction shorts. "You are one noisy son of a bitch lately," he said.

I nodded. "So?" I said.

"I'm just saying," he said. Then he put me through a hellacious kettlebell workout.

Not only didn't I cry, but I rocked it, man. Grandpa's right. Using anger to fuel a workout is killer, Mr. Rodriguez.

Two hours later, I had fifteen new messages on my Facebook post. By midafternoon, I had twenty-six.

The Geekers were becoming united. Sort of.

Strengthening the bone, I guess. The leadership bone.

Here's the problem: I didn't really have anything to tell any of the twenty-six band people who contacted me. So I wrote back to all of them. I'm putting together a plan of action. Stay tuned. This is the beginning.

Everybody was pretty cool, except Austin Bates, who wrote back to me, Can't wait to hear about your big plan, fudge nuts.

Camille had to go to her grandma's house to help her weed and crap, so she wasn't available for counsel.

No, didn't hear a peep out of Shaver. Why would Shaver contact me?

I know people think Shaver had something to do with all this, but other than falling apart and getting arrested, he didn't.

Justin was totally silent. Remember how he texted me a couple days before with Talk tomorrow? He didn't contact me at all. I'm sure he saw all the stuff on Facebook. He's the class president and he stays on top of everyone's business. Dude seriously knows if someone's grandma in Ohio has a cold or whatever. He wouldn't miss this band news just because he'd fallen in love with a magical evil witch.

Kailey? How would I know her reaction, man?

Okay. Sure. You already know apparently. Yes, I did get a Facebook message from Baba Obi that said I'm sorry. I'm sorry. I'm sorry.

No, sir, I don't mind if you use the facilities. Good luck to you. They aren't pretty.

CHAPTER 12

Welcome back, Mr. Rodriguez. You were gone a long time.

Talked to who?

Yeah! You'd think the cops would do a better job cleaning their bathroom. It's like they hired Doris to be the janitor or something. Better laugh than cry.

Way to change the subject by the way. Who did you talk to?

Fine. I'll tell you about Tuesday.

Resort people really started flowing into the donut shop on Tuesday morning. It's been a pretty cool start to the season, right? But the weather Tuesday got summery, temperature in the 80s (not great for a fat kid who sweats like a hot dog). The rich people swarmed, man. *Two Long Johns! Is this whole wheat? Do you use local ingredients? Half dozen of the glazed*—Gore and I were on, but Dante had to call RC III to come help too. That's how crazy it was.

While all the richies shouted about donuts, Camille texted me like ten times. She kept suggesting different places where we could have the concert. Wilson Beach on the sand, the playground next to the marina, softball field (which is actually in use throughout Spunk River Days), etc. Then she asked questions like Where are we going to practice? I drove up to school. It's locked. How can we get the sheet music? Music stands? How many songs do you think we all know by memory? Haven't marched or pepped in a long time.

At one point, even though customers were staring at me, I texted back TOO BUSY. TALK LATER.

RC III and Gore glared at me. Gore said, "Stop looking at your phone. Too many customers. You're not acting like a professional."

"Like a professional donut salesman? What's that?" I asked while I was pulling a jelly-filled donut for a blond kid.

The kid's mom smiled.

"Quality in all we do," Gore said.

"Hah," RC III laughed. "That's what my dad says."

"Quality in looking like a zombie," I mumbled.

"I heard that," Gore said. RC III glared at me and

shook his head. But Gore laughed a little. Gore doesn't ever let rip like a roaring laugh, but she actually laughs a lot. It's just sort of hard to tell. Her black lipstick mouth doesn't really smile. She just makes a little exhale sound and her eyes crinkle.

Did you know she has purple eyes?

Well, blue-violet anyway.

Man, we worked and worked and worked.

Around 10:30, the store emptied out, largely because Dante didn't have enough donuts made and our shelves were all pretty much bare (except for just the regular, unfrosted cakes, which aren't that tasty).

I lifted my apron up and wiped sweat off my face.

"Not smart, man," RC III said. "That's a dirty apron."

"You have icing on your forehead," Gore said.

I used my sweaty hand to wipe icing off my forehead. What a sticky mess. Donut work ain't easy work.

RC III made a face. "I'm going to go get you a wet towel," he said. He disappeared in back.

Gore leaned over the counter and took a deep breath. She didn't wear a Dante's T-shirt like RC III and I did. She wore a lacy blouse with the sleeves rolled up and a Dante's apron over the top.

"Who keeps texting you?" she asked. "Your girlfriend?"

"I don't have a girlfriend," I said.

"Camille," she said. "Is that who keeps texting?"

"Yeah."

"What does she want?"

"Jesus. Why do you care?" I spat.

"I don't know," Gore said. She swallowed hard. "Never mind."

RC III came from in back and tossed me a towel. He gave one to Gore too.

"No. Sorry," I said, wiping my face. "She wants to know where we should practice and where we should have the concert next weekend because it has to be a place around Wilson Beach where Spunk River people will actually show up."

"Go up to school," RC III said. "Practice there."

"It's locked up," I said.

"No," RC III said. "It's open in the afternoon for a couple hours."

"Oh," Gore said. Then she stood up straight. "Too bad you're such a jerk."

"I'm not a jerk," I said.

"No, dude! You a real ass to her," RC III said, pointing at Gore.

"I am?" I asked.

"You know there's a ballroom in my house?" Gore said.

Yeah. Gore lives in that giant Victorian place about two blocks up shore from Wilson Beach. Twin Cities richies used to build mansions instead of jamming themselves into little cabins and resorts.

Yes, sir. It's a cool place. Scary. Which is appropriate. I mean, that sort of adds to her legend, you know? Legend of the murder-crazed girl in the haunted house.

"Oh?" I said.

"So if you weren't such a jerk, I'd let you practice there. Dad isn't home this week."

"Wow. Okay. That's really, really nice of you," I said.

"I didn't offer anything, you jerk," Gore said. Then she went in back.

"Why are you so mean to her, man?" RC III said. "It's like you never learned common manners. Why would you pick on that girl?"

I paused for a second. "Ow," I said.

"Yeah, ow, man," RC III said.

Honestly, I didn't know I could be mean to anyone.

"Holy balls. I'm really, really sorry," I said to RC III.

"Don't tell me, dude."

"Right," I said. Then I ran outside and picked a bunch of dandelions off the strip between the sidewalk and the street. When Gore returned from in back, I handed her the bouquet.

She looked down at them. "Okay," she said.

"These are yours, okay, because I'm really, really sorry I'm a jerk."

"Nobody has ever given me flowers," Gore said.

"Well, they're yours."

Then Gore said really quietly, almost a whisper, "Your band can practice in our ballroom if you need to. I still think you're kind of a jerk though, even if I like you for no apparent reason."

"I wouldn't like you if I were her," RC III said to me.

"I don't like you," Gore said to RC III.

He smiled really big. "Come on. Yes, you do. You like me."

"Okay," Gore said. "I like you, but I don't want to because you're one of them."

"Are you racist?" I whispered.

"No, you dick," Gore shot back. "Robert is an athlete."

"She's an activity-ist," RC III said. "Prejudiced based on how a person spends his free time."

"Sports are dumb," Gore nodded. "And they attract bad people."

RC III was totally like…I think the word is tickled. He giggled like a little girl. Gore smiled back at him, sort of giggled too. They'd just worked one shift alone together, but Gore and RC III were clearly buddies. Talk about an odd couple.

Just then, a couple big families came cruising into the shop. "Do you have any gluten-free donuts?" a super skinny woman in sunglasses asked.

Gore smiled and said, "No, but we make all our products with extra, extra care."

"Oh," the woman said. "Good."

Right before close, Gore gave me her home phone number, said to call if we decided to use her house.

"I really appreciate it," I said.

"Thanks for the dandelions," she said quietly.

I called Camille before Dante locked up. Of course, she was a little skeptical about organizing a band practice at Gore's house. "I don't know. Will anyone go over there?" she asked.

CHAPTER 13

I was planning to go directly home so I could eat something healthy and fast (no donuts for my third straight day of work!) and then do my grandpa's workout. But RC III was waiting for me when I left the shop. He sat drinking a chocolate milk out on the picnic table under Dante's canopy.

"Dude, you want to see what the cheerleaders are doing?"

"Where?"

"Up at school. Bet they're there again."

"You saw them?"

"Heard them. Yesterday. About this time."

Man, I wanted to go home. I was so sticky and gross and I wanted to work out. But I felt sort of honored that RC III was taking an interest in my business. Know what I mean?

"What are they doing?" I asked.

"I don't know. I just heard the music, man. Let's go check it out. I'll give you a ride home after."

Five minutes later, we (both of us sticky) rolled into the MLAHS parking lot in RC III's black Honda. Sure enough, Kailey's Buick was out there in the lot. Janessa's SUV. A bunch of other cars were out there too. Just seeing those cars sent a shock of fear through me.

"Let's go in," RC III said.

"No," I said. "I don't want to—I don't need to know what's up."

"Why?" he asked.

"I…I don't want them to see me spying," I said.

"We'll just walk back through the commons, head to the locker room. I can say I'm picking up some laundry from my locker if anyone asks. You know you want to see this."

"Okay," I whispered.

I don't know why I was so freaked out by the notion that Kailey, Janessa, and Emily Yu might see me poking around. But I was. Terrified.

I followed RC III through the doors. My heart blasted. We entered the commons. The cheerleaders weren't in there. But then there was this thumping bass blasting through the gym doors and RC III just walked right over and opened a door right up, looked right in. I looked in under his arm and there they were, the dance team in short shorts and tiny T-shirts. And they were all humping and bumping to this… like, club music.

"What is this, the stripper team?" RC III asked.

"What? What?" I said. I jammed my head under his armpit for a better view.

Janessa, while she spun, saw us in the door. She stopped and waved at RC III. Then this tight-skirted, giant-haired, big-boobed blond lady I'd never seen before barked, "What do you boys think you are doing?" She had this thick Southern accent.

"Nothing, ma'am. Just heard the music," RC III replied.

"This is a closed practice, young man," she said.

Kailey smiled at RC III. Then she saw me and her smile faded fast.

Emily mouthed "Chunk?" in this really ugly way that made me boil.

I pushed past RC III and said, "Hi, ladies!"

"Get your big butt right back out that door," the

blond-haired woman cried. She ran toward us and her body just bounced in this awesome way, sir. Like beautiful. Like I can visualize it in slow motion.

RC III grabbed the back of my donut shirt and pulled me through into the commons. The door slammed in our faces.

"Who the hell was that woman?" I asked.

"Their coach," RC III said.

"Wow. She's…she's pretty hot," I said.

"Don't think with your groin, man. She's your enemy."

"Okay, but she's the hottest mom I've ever seen."

"I bet she's expensive."

His statement confused me because I was all lit up by her in a weird way. "What?" I whispered, "You think she's a prostitute?"

"Dude." RC III spoke slowly to me like I'm an idiot, which I am. "She's the cheerleader's new coach and she's probably the reason the school can't afford your band."

"Oh," I said. The truth of the matter dawned on me. "The school replaced Shaver with her."

RC III nodded. "Yeah, man. Seems like it."

"She's…she's beautiful."

"Dude! You're a horndog! She's the enemy!"

A minute later, we were back in RC III's car. He pulled out of the lot. I thought about Big Boobs. The buzz I got from her began to wear off. "That woman replaced Shaver, but I thought I loved her," I whispered.

"Candy," RC III said. "She's a glazed donut, dude."

"She's the enemy," I said. "She took band."

"Don't let them fool you," RC III nodded.

"She's the enemy," I repeated. "What's wrong with me?"

"Same thing that's wrong with most people," RC III said.

"I want all the donuts in my mouth no matter how bad they are for me."

We drove for a while in silence. Then RC III said, "I don't know about this concert thing you guys want to do. Takes too much planning. Seems like you should be more aggressive anyway. You should get in the cheerleaders' faces a little more. Make more of a public display. Disrupt their shit a little."

"Really? How?" I asked.

"I don't know. Just think about it."

We got to my house. "Okay. But we need to raise some cash for camp."

"Whatever you think, dude. See you tomorrow," RC III said. Then he fist-bumped me and I felt pretty damn cool, sir. RC III is far more awesome than Justin Cornell.

Grandpa was waiting for me at the door, already wearing his compaction shorts. (Yes, RC III saw him.) "Look at you, fancy pants. Getting dropped off by the school quarterback in his fancy-pants car."

"I think it's a Honda Civic."

"It's a fancy-pants Civic."

"Okay," I said.

"Time for the circuit of hell."

And while Grandpa killed me with the burpees and crap, I thought it might be nice to have some club music thumping to help me keep my energy up. I thought, *Wish that big-boobed blond lady were barking at me. Wish Kailey were here dancing—*

I have problems, sir. I think cheerleaders are hot. Even mom-aged cheerleaders who bark like wild dogs. I'm a glazed donut addict.

When we finished, Dad was home, sitting at the dinner table, although there was no dinner yet made.

"What are you two up to?" he asked.

Sweat soaked my donut shirt and my stretchy pants. (I hadn't changed.) "Nothing," I said.

"Oh, no," he said. "You're doing something."

I need something to drink, Mr. Rodriguez. I'm sorry. I don't want to be a pain in the ass.

Unsweetened iced tea or a glass of water. Nothing with sugar, okay?

CHAPTER 14

Thanks. That tea hit the spot.

Okay. When he said, "Oh, no, you're doing something," I had to tell Dad something because I didn't want him to know I was exercising, which I know doesn't make any sense, except I was worried he'd want to join in. He'd stink up the joint. He'd start and do it for a couple days. Then he'd quit exercising. Then I'd quit and then we'd eat a thousand tacos. And I'd feel hopeless again, which for some reason I didn't, even though some bad stuff was going on.

Instead of telling Dad about Project Kill Chunk, I told him about the lack of band camp, about the pop machine. He was almost interested! Like, for twenty seconds, he listened! Dad's opinion? "You need to write a letter to the editor," he said. "People in town will be upset if they know what's happening. Might get some support."

Then he ate a couple sandwiches. (Grandpa didn't cook because our workout got in the way of his cooking schedule.) Then Dad watched *Pawn Stars.*

I sat at the table after Dad left. Grandpa cleaned up around me. He asked, "What are you stewing on?"

"Dad's right, right? I should write a letter to the paper."

"Seems reasonable," Grandpa said.

"It does."

Generally, I think of Dad as being such a loser. I'd never pay attention to his advice. (Look what he's done for us so far—chased Mom away, gotten us fat as hell, gotten us an old man to live in our house.) I could complain about bad government and notify the community about the upcoming concert too!

So instead of watching TV, I went downstairs and sent a message to Ms. Feagan asking her for an example of a good letter to the editor. She sent me a few and wrote I believe I know what you're upset about and I'm completely on your side, Gabe. Let me know if I can be of further assistance. That made me feel great! So I grabbed my laptop, stretched out on my bed, and wrote a letter, copying the kind of language that was in Ms. Feagan's examples. I worked so hard on it. I tried to channel my inner Justin Cornell. I tried to sound so balanced and smart and true.

Yeah, it's in my email. So is Friesen's response. Let me pull it up.

June 11

Dear Good People of Minnekota:

Democracy does not function behind closed doors. Democracy only works in the full light of the day when all interested parties are deemed worthy of notification and participation. In the case of the school district's recent repricing of vending machine items and the subsequent redistribution of vending machine profits, democracy failed.

Without warning or discussion, the Minnekota Lake Area High School band lost its vending money, the money that funds summer programs. At the same time, Minnekota Lake Area High School cheer-leading received said monies for the purposes of creating a new dance team. While I do not argue against the introduction of new programming at the school and would never say that cheerleading is anything but a wonderful and vital aspect of the student extracurricular community, I do argue with the behind-closed-doors process that resulted in this action and the subsequent alcohol-fueled arrest of Mr. Shaver, the band teacher.

Changes affect real people (Mr. Shaver and the children).

If changes are to be made, if resources are to be redistributed, as is often necessary, let the changes be brought before the stakeholders and let the community determine what is and what isn't of value.

For now, the band is fending for itself (hopefully) by doing a live concert during Spunk River Days, date and time TBA. Be there to support your hometown band like we support the football and basketball teams!

Sincerely,
Gabriel Johnson
MLAHS Class of 2015

It was about 8 p.m. when I finished and I rolled out of the bed and stretched and blinked. Then I carried my computer upstairs to show the letter to Dad and Grandpa.

Dad was snoring in his chair. Grandpa sat at the kitchen table reading a *Cooking Light* magazine.

"Hey, will you read this over for me? I have to send it in by midnight to get it in Thursday's paper."

"Uh-huh. Yup," Grandpa said.

I put the computer in front of him. He stared at it for about five minutes, which seemed a little long. He blinked. Sniffed. Then said, "You're a hell of a smart kid. That's good. That's just plain good, Chunk."

"All right," I said. "Thanks, Grandpa!"

"Doesn't mean that jackass Friesen will print it. Man comes from a long line of pissants and assholes. Just be aware of that fact."

"He'll print it. What's he got to lose?" I said.

"Kaus advertising bucks," Grandpa said.

"Oh." I thought for a second. But weren't papers required to print opinion letters? Wasn't that their job? "Well, I tried to be respectful," I said.

"It's a good letter, Gabe."

I went back downstairs, took a big breath, felt all proud and powerful and right and good. Then I fired the letter to BFriesen@MLJournal.com and that bastard wrote me back in like ten seconds! This is what he wrote:

Chunk,

Nice try. We have a representative democracy. We elect a school board, so it makes the important decisions for our community. The school board decided about the pop machine. I should know because I was at the meeting, so I was part of the situation over there. And I know Shaver is sad and in a pile of trouble now, but that is his own fault for not acting like an upstanding man. Sorry I can't print your letter because you do not understand the nature of government. We should fire your teachers.

Sincerely,
Bob Friesen

Okay, sir. You know who's a total idiot?

That's right! Bob Friesen! He's the *publisher* of the

local *newspaper* and he doesn't know anything about *government*! My teachers, especially Mr. March in eighth grade, taught me plenty about government. There's an open meeting law in Minnesota that requires school boards to announce not only the time and place of the meeting but what's going to be on the agenda so community members can make statements for or against what's being voted on (took me ten seconds to verify on Google). They posted the meeting about defunding the fall play. Because of Ms. Feagan, everybody went to the meeting to tell them no!

Friesen is a jerk. Representational democracy? Holy balls, I know what that is! I'm not stupid. Bob Friesen wouldn't publish my letter because…because—

Money.

Yeah, he's Kaus's golf buddy too. At least, he used to be. Things are changing with the Kauses.

Oh, balls, was I pissed.

I ran upstairs and told Grandpa what happened.

He nodded and smirked. "Yup," he said.

"Who do I report this to? Who can I complain to?"

"Hell if I know. Ask your dad in the morning. He might have an idea."

"Damn," I said.

I trudged back downstairs and jumped on my bed and called Camille to tell her about this outrage!

Her reaction wasn't what I was expecting. She said, "You didn't tell me you were going to write a letter, Chunk. I should be the one writing the letters."

"Why is that?" I asked.

"Well, I'm the smart one. Everybody will think we're just joking if you write letters."

"Oh, yeah?" I said.

"Yeah," she said.

"Oh, really?" I said.

"Can I post on Facebook that we're going to have a practice at Gore's house tomorrow?" Camille asked.

"Great," I said. "Fine. You'd better do that so I don't screw it up and tell people we're practicing in the lake or something because I'm so dumb."

"Don't be a sour apple," Camille said.

Is this stuff black iced tea, Mr. Rodriguez? I mean, caffeinated iced tea?

I feel weird.

Because I don't know if you've noticed, but my mouth is going really, really fast and I feel a little bit jumpy like maybe I just drank several coffees or Dews or whatever in a very short time. And I was so thirsty I think I've sucked down like four glasses of that iced tea and *man*. Look at my hand! My hand is waving around fast! Look at that sick speed! I think my heart's beating too fast!

CHAPTER 15

I'm better. I'm okay. I wish I could go outside. Fresh air. I could use some fresh air.

Okay.

Camille posted an announcement on Facebook about practicing for this stupid Spunk River concert that wasn't really scheduled and lots of people decided they would show up at Gore's house, which surprised me and also clearly surprised Gore.

I called her at her house from Dante's the next morning because she didn't work with me on Wednesday. I gave her the list of band peeps who were going to attend. She was excited and sort of pissed. "But I hate all those people and now they're coming over?"

"You volunteered," I said.

"I'll grill some hamburgers," she said. "Dad ordered like ten pounds of grass-fed beef. It's tasty. Everyone will like it. Except for the vegetarians. Is anyone a vegetarian? I'm thinking about being a vegetarian."

"I don't know."

"I'll grill veggie burgers too. I made my own with dried mushrooms and black beans. They're good."

"Sweet. Thanks," I said.

"Holy cow! I don't like any of those people," she said. Then she hung up.

Goth girl says holy cow. Ha-ha.

After the shop closed, me and RC III sat down at the picnic table out front, which was becoming like our office because we sat out there so much. RC III brought a whole box of leftover bismarcks. (Dante overproduced donuts because the morning before was so crazy.)

RC III opened it and grabbed a jelly-filled one and then offered the box to me.

"No, thanks," I said.

"Really?" he asked.

"Can't. Those things will make you fat," I said.

"True. If you eat too many of them."

"Every day, which is what I've been doing for the last couple years."

"Well, not lately. You dropping weight?" RC III asked.

Okay, Mr. R. Okay. This question filled me with such instant pride I can't even tell you. I had been in huge pain and exhausted for almost five days. I hadn't broken though. I ate no donuts. No pop. I barely had a third of the dinner I usually ate. I'd worked out…hard. And yes, that morning, when I pulled on my damn stretchy pants, they felt a little loose in the midsection.

Like the stretch didn't have to stretch so far.

"A little," I said, nodding. "Working out with my grandpa."

"Your grandpa in his jock strap at the door? Weird, dude," RC III said.

"Yeah. Totally."

Awesome he mentioned dropping weight because that was enough for me to look those donuts in the eye and say, *You're not going down the hole, chocolate friends.*

Then he asked me about Gore; "She have a boyfriend or anything?"

"I don't know what she does," I said.

"She's cool," he said.

"I guess," I said.

"You like her?"

"No!" I said. "Remember? I'm mean to her."

"Chill. Just asking, man," he said. "Watched you on the phone with her. Your face was all lit up."

"What do you mean 'lit up'?"

"Smiley. You going to her house tonight?"

"Uh. Yeah. Everybody. Because—" I got all tongue-tied because I suddenly wondered if I loved Gore. I'm crazy. "Just because she volunteered her house. Guess we'll put her ballroom to use. We have to practice for our nonexistent concert, you know."

"Uh-huh. Did you come up with any better strategies? I fear for that concert."

Then I told him the story about my letter to the editor and he shook his head.

"So much for free press, man."

"I know. Blows my mind," I said.

"You know what? I think you should have a protest."

"Ha-ha."

"Why are you laughing?" he asked.

"Are you kidding?"

"No, this town is backward and inbred and shit. Needs some shaking up. You should protest those cheerleaders and that new candy coach of theirs right up in their faces."

I thought about it. *He's right, right?* Then I pictured me with super long hair and Camille in her hippie pants playing tambourine, singing *We shall overcome* to the cheerleaders. "That's pretty funny," I said.

"How is that funny?" he asked.

"Like, if they had evil corporate cheerleader offices and we'd come and camp out in their plaza and smoke weed and play Hacky Sack and guitar and bongos and crap. Hilarious."

"First, my grandfather was part of the civil rights movement and he'd be pretty offended by what you describe as a protest."

"Oh, sorry."

RC III stood up. He was jacked. "Second, those girls have already occupied your summer program. That crazy-ass coach is up at your school, squawking at them like she belongs. Don't you think they should know the pain they're causing you all? The pain of occupation?"

"Maybe—" I said.

"Uh-huh. I'm right."

"You are?"

"Mind if I come over for your practice tonight?" he asked.

"No." Then I shook my head. "You want to come to band practice. Really?"

"Yeah, I'm curious about your band."

"You know we're like a marching band, not a rock band, right?"

"Uh, dude, I heard you play a lot last year. I'm in sports, you know?"

"No. I had no idea!" I said. "You? You're so small and out of shape!"

RC III laughed his *hehe* giggle laugh. "You farmer kids crack me up, man."

"I'm not funny," I said. But I got a little burst of adrenaline. If RC III showed up at the band rehearsal, people might think we're friends.

Whoa. I just said that out loud, Mr. Rodriguez. I want you to know that I know saying that out loud makes me sound like a big superficial idiot, okay? I'm telling you the truth about everything because clearly a liar would try to hide the fact that he's so superficial and dumb, right?

At the time, I thought RC III wanted to go to the practice because he was hot for Gore, but I think he actually really likes nerds generally.

CHAPTER 16

After work, I walked in the door and found Dad lying on the couch, eating some Italian cheese bread, which I like. Italian cheese bread is one of the better things Dad makes. (He doesn't make much, Mr. R.) "I left you a couple slices in the oven, Gabe," he said. My heart began to beat a little heavy. My mouth watered. Like a zombie looking for flesh, I hobbled into the kitchen. I pulled the oven door open and took a big whiff. Oh, the sweet smell of melted butter and mozzarella on French bread. Without a thought in my head, I reached out for a slice and then received a blow to the shoulder, which made me cry out in pain.

I quickly turned to punch out whoever had done this to me. (Really, I meant to punch.) Grandpa stood there shirtless, a snarl on his lips. In his right hand, he carried a small, red-and-white, speedo-like swimsuit. "Put this on," he whispered. "We're going to the river."

"Why?" I whispered back.

"Your old man took the day off so he could stay home and keep an eye on us."

"Eye?"

"Spying. You want a workout?"

"Yeah," I said, staring at the swimsuit.

"Strap this sucker on your nuggets."

"I don't know, Grandpa," I whispered.

"Do you even have a pair of shorts you fit into?"

"No."

"Then you'd better do as I say or we're going to have to skip today—unless you want your old man to know you're working out, which is fine by me."

Yeah. Tiny suit. I still find it hard to believe I agreed. Back in the day, I was a pretty good swimmer. I did summer swim team with Justin for a few summers, but I hadn't been in water other than the shower for a couple of years (and I sure didn't want to wear any swimsuit, much less a damn banana hammock swimsuit). But I thought about RC III asking me if I'd lost some weight and I really didn't want to miss a workout. And I didn't want to be in the house with that cheese bread and I really didn't want

Dad involved. Stupid, maybe. But I did it. Wrapped that sucker around my nuggets.

Stupid in that it caused me trouble. Maybe because in the end, who gives a crap about Seth Sellers and mean people? Who cares what they think?

I went down to the basement and pulled on this red-and-white checkered suit, which was as small as they come. I think the thing was something Grandpa wore in the 70s when he was a little bit bigger. It slid up over my thighs okay. (Grandpa had giant body-builder thighs back in the day.) But my waist is pretty dang big. I tied the thing and it settled under my gut. I looked in the mirror and I looked like one of those inflatable clown punching bags for kids with a rubber band wrapped around the middle. I bulged out on either side. Big time. "Oh, man," I said. I pulled my stretchy pants on over the top and grabbed my hoodie and climbed the stairs. Felt like I was losing blood flow to my wang area. Not pretty.

Grandpa met me at the top of the stairs. He carried a duffel bag. He wore his giant old-man sunglasses. He called out to the living room, "Me and Chunk are going for groceries. You need anything?"

Dad was clearly snoozing. "What?" he mumbled back.

"Groceries," Grandpa said.

"Good, good," Dad said.

Grandpa went out through the back door and then crept around the side of the house. I followed, sort of ducking, I guess to stay out of sight. We jogged to the front where Grandpa parks his orange van, which he's had for my entire life. It's a 1980s Chevy. It has ripped-up seats. It sounds like a construction site when it runs, which it doesn't very often because Grandpa doesn't leave the house much, only for groceries (or to take me to school the couple times I was late).

When we were both in, Grandpa said, "Spunk River Challenge. Used to do this when I was a kid." He turned the key. The van exploded with noise. We took off. There are no seatbelts in this van, sir, which is highly illegal.

We drove through town, scaring children with the violent noise. (We made a toddler cover his ears and cry on Park Street. The mom glared at us.) We parked at the far edge of the lot at Wilson Beach near the mouth of the Spunk River.

"We can't swim here," I said.

"Sure we can," Grandpa replied. "Current makes you work hard."

"People are going to see me," I said.

"So?" Grandpa said. "What's your problem?"

"My problem is I'm a blimp," I said.

"Get over yourself," Grandpa said. "Nobody gives a damn but you."

"Yeah. Right."

I was very, very nervous and jumpy pulling off my pants and hoodie, but I did it. I'm glad I did it. Take back the night. Reclaim Gabe!

Grandpa (wearing a silver suit so tiny it was pretty much a thong) waded right in and he's all muscle, so he's kind of a sinker. He took a couple steps and *boom*—he was under. I cried out and then jumped in after him. As soon as I hit the water, Grandpa's head popped out from under the surface. He spit water out of his mouth and said, "Stroke it, boy!" Then he took off dog-paddling. I know how to freestyle and I passed by his ass really easily.

The river is not huge, right? It's what…maybe twenty yards across at Wilson? Well, I beat the old man across by about ten yards. He shouted, "Give her another run!" So I pushed off the muddy bottom and swam back. About midway through, my muscles started burning and I stopped and took in a big breath and sucked some water in and coughed a bunch and panicked for a second and then thought, *Dude, you're like ten feet from where you can walk. Don't be a wuss.* It's not like the Spunk is super deep. The lake drops off pretty fast, but no matter what, ten yards just isn't that big a deal. So I swam another four or five strokes and got to the edge and I felt awesome. It took Grandpa about five minutes to turn around and come back to my side.

"Let's do her again."

I did. And my muscles burned more and the current pushed me. But I just kept kicking. And the sun beat down on the water and birds flew by in the sky. And back and forth I went another time.

The third time I honestly thought I might die. (Not really, not exactly, but I was dousing out like a late-night campfire.) It took me a long time to swim that one, my heart crushing out thuds in my chest, and Grandpa totally kept up with me, doing his dog-paddle spittle swimming. He must've swallowed a couple gallons of that gross water because by the end of the third back-and-forth, he was pretty cashed.

"Good boy. Good work, Chunk," he coughed.

We had to sort of slide up the banks on our bellies and we got pretty muddy. And once we got out, Grandpa coughed and threw up a bunch of water on the grass. That's gross.

He stood up straight, put his hands on his hips, coughed some more, and then laughed. "Hell's bells," he said.

"Are you okay?" I asked.

"I don't know how to swim too good. But I knew you liked it," he said.

"I do," I said. "That was super fun," I gasped.

"Mind if we lie down for a minute?"

Grandpa pulled a couple towels out of the duffel bag he'd brought. We spread them out on the ground and I spread-eagled on my back. The sun beat down on my flesh (for the first time in years), and unfortunately, I was asleep within seconds. Swimming is tough.

I wouldn't have gone to sleep if I thought anyone was around. We were too close to the maintenance shed. Easy to see for city park workers like Seth Sellers, who has a summer job with the city. He's silent like an assassin. He didn't wake us up anyway. Seth Sellers posted a picture that afternoon. "Beached Whale and Donkey Man asleep in park."

I wish I'd at least pulled on my hoodie, you know? But the sun felt really good. I've missed the sun.

When we got home, Dad said, "Where are the groceries?"

Grandpa stumbled around for words. Then I said, "Well, I'll be damned. We left them in the cart."

"You were gone for two hours," Dad said.

"You were asleep, you lazy ass," Grandpa said. "We were gone a half hour."

"Oh, really?" Dad said.

We had to climb back into Grandpa's shit mobile to go back to the store. The mud on my belly was itchy as hell.

Dad was totally suspicious. What a jerk.

At least it absorbed enough time in the afternoon that I didn't have time to look at my computer. I don't know if I'd have gone to Gore's house with that Facebook humiliation hanging over my head.

Beached whale.

Hey, Mr. Rodriguez, there's a dude at the door.

CHAPTER 17

What did Chief Bartell have to say? Does he think I'll get the electric chair?

Yeah, thank God we don't have capital punishment in Minnesota! People really hate pop machine robbers. *Die, pop robber! Zap!*

The case is developing? That sounds a little scary, okay? What do you mean?

I'm telling you the whole story.

Yes, I am. If you know something I don't, you should say it!

Fine. We met at Gore's that afternoon. Camille picked me up.

Yes, sir, it is a castle. Big old pointy turret Victorian castle. It's pretty freaky really. Scary if you're scared by stuff like that. (Tess Cook, for example, is totally freaked out by old-castle-looking places apparently.)

Why would you live in a place like that when there

are only two of you? Just Mr. Wettlinger and Gore in there? There are like eight bedrooms and five bathrooms!

Yes, they have parties. And there always seems to be people visiting from out of town. I saw a group on Friday. Gore's dad is gay obviously. It's not like a big secret or anything. He has old-man dance parties. I've been to one now.

I'm a pretty great dancer, sir.

In any case, the point is this: Between Camille's invitation and my freak-out post about how we're all idiots, lots of band peeps were motivated to show up at the meeting.

Wow, you have a list of attendees?

Yes, that's everybody, I think. All the original Geekers. The police do good work.

No, RC III wasn't there. He couldn't. He texted that he got in a fight with his dad, so he had to stay in for the night. He doesn't really belong anyway, you know? He's not a Geeker. Not by any stretch, man. He's a jock.

J. D. Carlson? Are you kidding?

No, J. D. Carlson wasn't there. He had nothing to do with this. He's a crazy loser. Totally on drugs.

He was caught breaking into pop machines last night? Huh. Really?

I think he did that on his own then. Random coincidence?

Well, a couple big things happened while I was out swimming, sleeping, and buying grub with Grandpa. First, Seth Sellers posted the picture of me wearing a tiny checkered swimsuit on Facebook. So that was great. Second, word started to spread around Minnekota that the school board was meeting on Friday afternoon to discuss the possible dismissal of Mr. Shaver.

The dude did it to himself, you know? Drive around drunk in this little town? Come on! Problem is, he's a nice guy and a great band teacher, so this hurt.

Camille and I got to Gore's first. We rang the bell (sounded like a church bell bonging). Gore opened the door, didn't smile, nodded, and turned and we followed her back through the giant house—big foyer, living room with giant fireplace, and giant leather couches attached to an open kitchen. (They had clearly remodeled the hell out of the place. Mom used to watch a lot of HGTV, so I recognized the quality appliances and crap.) Then we went out a deck door to the back, which has docks and looks over the lake.

"Dang," Camille said. "I thought our farm was pretty."

"Your farm is pretty," Gore said. "I've seen it."

"Oh?" Camille asked.

"You want some chips? Lemonade?" Gore gestured to a cooler with her spatula.

I walked over and got a lemonade. Camille sat down and stared out at the lake.

Gore stood over sizzling meat, totally grilling up a storm, which looked funny as hell because she was wearing a black dress that went all the way to her feet and thick black eyeliner and lipstick and she'd totally pancaked her face white as a ghost. Because I'd seen her a few times at Dante's wearing an apron, the full regalia was pretty startling, especially as she was grilling hamburgers in it.

Without looking at us, Gore said, "So that picture of Gabe. Attempt at crushing you, huh?"

"Oh," Camille sat up straight. "Yeah. It's pretty bad. What were you doing lying around on the ground like that, Chunk?" she asked.

I popped open the lemonade and took a sip. "When? What?"

"When Seth Sellers took that picture of you and your grandpa in your shiny underpants," Camille said.

"What?" I shouted.

"Crap. Okay. I thought you were avoiding the topic. That's why I didn't mention it in the car," Camille said. "Chunk, um, I'm sorry to say that you're an MLAHS Facebook sensation."

"Seth Sellers is a bad person," Gore said without any noticeable emotion. "My computer's on the counter." She pointed at a laptop sitting on a stone counter across the deck. "Take a look, Gabe."

I already wanted to throw up. I already knew what I looked like in that stupid banana hammock. Like a freaking inflatable clown. I also knew Grandpa was wearing a silver thong and I knew we were covered in mud. We also fell asleep right next to each other in full view of the world. What was I thinking, sir?

No, I didn't want to see the picture itself. I wanted to see who was commenting. I wanted to see what they were saying.

Big white whale me asleep on the towel next to mostly naked grandfather. Good God, sir. Jesus.

There were dozens of comments. Mean and nasty,

man. I scanned for Justin's name in the comments. If he said something mean, I'd be forced to hate him forever.

All the beached gay whale and pig boy and donkey man insults came from jocks and cheerleaders (and Austin Bates, who is in the freaking band). Mostly, it was Seth, Emily Yu, and Janessa writing back and forth. Justin didn't write anything. I had to check the "likes." There were twenty-five. And yeah, Justin Cornell, my best friend, "liked" the humiliating picture. My stomach tightened into a walnut. I pulled out my phone and texted him, You are dead to me.

He texted back Why? Because I won't play in your stupid fund-raiser for our alcoholic band teacher? So sorry.

No, I wrote, because you're a bad person. Take care.

Whatever, Chunk. That's all he wrote. The walnut slid up to my throat.

"You know what," I said to Camille. "Screw this. Screw these people."

"Yeah," she said.

I bent over because I couldn't breathe. Then the doorbell rang. I stood up straight. "Screw Justin," I said.

A few minutes later our numbers had grown to thirteen—Tess Cook and Austin Bates (the reprobate) and the Petersen girls and Omar Fulwider and others. Everybody had their instruments (except Austin and Omar, who are drummers, so their stuff is locked in the school). And everyone wanted to talk about the damn picture. Tess said, "I think it's cute that you and your grandpa can be naked together."

Austin Bates said, "Jelly donut." Then he laughed. That's what his comment on the Facebook page said too.

Schae Petersen said, "Seth Sellers is such a paltry excuse for a human."

I listened to them all talk, shook my head, bit my lip, considered ass-dancing because that's what I'd done in the past to alleviate the stress. Then I swallowed hard and said, "I should've been naked. I'm so embarrassed."

"What, Gabe?" Gore asked.

"Me and my grandpa are petitioning to make Wilson a nude beach because our boys need fresh air, you know? We were protesting, but we lost our nerve. Grandpa didn't want us to get arrested."

They all stared at me for a second. Then Austin said, "Wilson nude? That'd be sweet, y'all. I want to enjoy my nakedness." He pulled off his shirt, so all he was wearing was the bandanna on his head and his giant rapper-sagging shorts. Last thing I wanted to see.

"You'd really go naked?" Gore asked. "At Wilson Beach?"

I nodded. "Hell yeah. I'm comfortable with my body."

"I wouldn't be if I was you, but that's cool," Austin said.

"I wouldn't be if I was you, man," Omar said. "You have the body of a homeless dog. Skin and tendons. Pretty gross."

"What, dude? I work for this shit," Austin shouted. Then he flexed. "I celebrate myself!" Then he ran toward the lake and leapt off the dock into the water.

Tess stripped off her shorts and shirt and chased him wearing her bra and underpants. Splash. She was in the water. Girl has been after Austin since kindergarten. Only the sweet Lord knows why, sir.

Gore said, "I'm going to be really mad if anyone drowns."

"Don't worry," I said. "I'm a very strong swimmer."

"You are?" Camille said. "When do you swim, Chunk?"

"All the time, girlfriend," I said.

And then I did it, sir. I peeled off my shirt and raised my arms above my head, letting my big gut expand in all its terrible glory. Omar started chanting, "Chunk, Chunk, Chunk." Then the Petersens chanted and I cupped my ear and stared at Camille and then at Gore. Gore chanted (more whispered), "Chunk, Chunk, Chunk." Camille just stared back at me.

I did my little ass-dance, which felt powerful, not stupid, and everybody laughed but in a good way. "I'm in," I said. I pulled off my stretchies, revealing my plaid boxers. Kicked off my shoes. I walked out to the dock and dove like a sweet swan into the lake.

Whale or not, nobody is going to take my dignity. No more.

No, I'm fully capable of taking my own dignity. But no one else is going to take it.

We got off to a pretty rousing start. Everybody but Camille and Gore stripped to their undies and jumped in the freaking lake and splashed around. It was great, man. It was awesome. There's a lot of freedom in just saying "This is my giant ass. Deal with it."

Ten minutes after we all jumped in, Camille walked out to the dock and said, "Gore's hamburgers are getting cold. We'd better eat them. Don't want her getting mad at us." She drew her finger across her neck like we might get our throats cut. Everybody climbed out fast.

Gore gave us towels. She did her "kind of" smile. I could tell she was having a good time. Everybody treated her like it was normal that we'd be there, even though I'm guessing nobody had talked to her in years. We ate out on the deck.

Oh, no, I'm not that great with myself. I dried off and pulled on my shirt right away. I'm not really interested in hanging at a nude beach, man. I'm psyched people think I want to though.

The late-day sun hovered over the lake. Gore played pretty cool music from her computer. A bunch of seagulls flew around in the sky. A couple pelicans scooped fish. They don't stay around here for long. I like them. I felt awesome

That's when Omar said, "Think Shaver is going to get fired?"

Austin said, "No. Everybody around here drunk drives."

"No, they don't," Camille said. "That's stupid."

Austin pursed his lips and nodded. "Oh, they

do, yo. Just don't beep their horn and shout at people outside the Kwik Trip like Shaver did the other night."

"That's what he did?" I asked.

"Yeah, dog," Austin said.

"That's why the school board is meeting Friday," Omar said. "To decide if they are going to fire him for acting so crazy."

Sir, apparently a lot can go down when you're sunning yourself in a banana hammock next to a river. I had no idea about this.

Yeah, Camille knew. So did Gore.

Speedboats began buzzing heavy on the lake. You know, the evening is always thick with boaters. "Can we please go inside? I need to speak to you guys," I said. "Too much noise."

We all went in except for Austin and Tess. Tess said she was scared of the house. (She's a kid at heart.) They stood at the screen door. Everyone else gathered on the big couches around the fireplace. Everyone but Camille. She stood up next to me, which is fair, right? She sent out the invitation.

Before I could start talking, she said, "So we're

gathered together today for a special reason. We are just five days from the beginning of band camp."

Austin shouted from the door, "There is no band camp. The school canceled our asses and our teacher got lit up like monkey, girl. Wake up."

"From the traditional beginning of camp. Usually. When we usually begin camp, okay?" she said.

We nodded. I wasn't sure where she was going. But I nodded, sir.

"We have decided to play a fund-raising concert for the band during Spunk River Days. That's why we're here."

"Wall of Sound plays on Sunday night at Spunk River Days. Can't believe they're coming here. Randall Andersson is freaking genius," Omar said.

Camille got a little flummoxed. "I know Wall of Sound is cool and I know the lake is pretty. And Chunk is fat and that's funny and everything. But we need to get organized to play our concert, okay?"

A few things occurred to me rapid-fire while Camille was speaking, Mr. Rodriguez. One, it's not funny that I'm fat. It's a fact, but it isn't funny. *Screw you, Camille.* Two, this concert idea was totally lame.

People at Spunk River Days want to see Wall of Sound, not a marching band. Plus, if Shaver was going to get fired, we'd really be raising money for nothing. There'd be no camp no matter what. Three, RC III was totally right. We should be more aggressive.

"Right," I said, breaking in. "Also, we need to show the school that we're not a bunch of losers and we're a force to be reckoned with."

"Hell yeah," Austin shouted from the screen door.

Camille broke back, "The concert will do that, so—"

"What if we protested that dance squad?" I asked.

"Protested?" Schae Petersen said. "Like with signs and…and marching?"

"Maybe," I said.

"I know," Austin said. "We could protest it Chunk-style. Get all naked and take pictures in the girls' locker room!"

"No," Camille said.

"Or break into Kailey's mama's dance school, yo. We could trash it," Austin cried.

"That's ridiculous. We don't have to be criminals about this," Camille said. "We just need to play our—"

"Did you guys know the dance squad has this new

coach and they're up at the high school in the gym all week? Me and RC III watched them practice yesterday," I said.

"You and RC III?" Camille asked. She shook her head like she couldn't comprehend the connection.

"Yeah, the school's replaced band camp with this stripper camp for cheerleaders. That's what it looked like."

"Cool," Austin said. Tess punched his arm.

"Why didn't you tell me you'd gone up there?" Camille asked.

I didn't talk to her. I talked to the band peeps. I leaned forward really intensely. "How many of you saw my Facebook post the other day? About the pop machine?"

Most people raised their hands—but not everybody.

"Listen, you guys. This is serious. This is straight-up serious, okay? The absolute, 100 percent reason we don't have camp is that the school board took all the money from the pop machine in the cafeteria and gave it to this dance coach to pay for the cheerleaders' stripper lessons."

"No!" Omar shouted.

"Is that really true?" Schae asked.

"Hell yeah, it is," I said.

"I only plug that bitch machine because we get the damn money back!" Austin shouted.

I think Austin drank as much Code Red as me during the school year, sir. He bought three bottles during our research project. (He didn't get fat though, lucky guy. He might be on meth, but I don't think he is.)

"Me too, dude," I said.

"That's why we're fund-raising," Camille said.

"Wow. Wow. No wonder Shaver went off the deep end," Schae said.

"Bet he got depressed because we get so little respect," Omar said.

"I want to blow some shit up!" Austin shouted.

"Yeah. Me too," Schae said.

Others sort of growled and got mad, which is good because we should be mad. We shouldn't just accept crap because we're used to crap, right?

"So what if we went up to the school tomorrow and did a little protesting? Let Deevers and the cheer bitches know that we're pissed and that Shaver had better not get fired and we're not going to take it."

"Don't call them bitches," Gore said, but nobody listened.

"And what if we get in trouble?" Camille asked.

"We'll use the trouble to spread word about the benefit concert. How about that?"

"Oh," Camille said.

"Sounds like a plan to me," Omar said.

"Yeah, we're in," Schae said, referring to herself and her twin sister, Caitlin, who never says a word. (She smiles really nice though.)

"We can't just show up at school," Camille said. "If we're going to protest, we have to make some signs and know what kinds of slogans we're going to shout."

"Really? Slogans?" Gore asked. "Like cheers?"

"Like cheers—but with a real message. 'No blood for oil!' or something."

"Whose blood?" Austin shouted from the door.

"Yeah!" Tess demanded.

"That's just an example," Camille said. "We need to make up cheers about how we're mad at—"

"Cheerleaders?" Schae said.

"How about this!" I said. "How about this?" I repeated because I thought I'd been struck by the freaking hand of God right in my face. "We don't talk. We don't cheer. We keep dead silent because they took away the music. Get it? And if the school fires Shaver, the music will die forever. We go in there and just stare at them in complete silence!"

"Really?" Camille asked. Her eyebrows were all knotted, her face pinched. "We just stare at them?"

"Yes! That's one spooky-ass protest, don't you think?" I said, excited.

"Maybe?" Gore said.

But everyone else thought that was a good idea. They all shouted, "Yeah!" and "Spooky." Camille totally rolled her eyes but didn't fight it.

So we had a plan!

Everyone agreed to do it too, even Gore, who has no connection to the band whatsoever except she hosted the practice, which turned out not to be a practice. We decided to meet at the school at 2:15. (RC III said the doors were open from 2 to 4 p.m. daily so football players could lift weights.) We decided we wouldn't say anything, that we'd be totally silent and spooky to show they'd taken away the music! Cool, right?

Yeah, not very effective maybe.

The only thing musical that was established during

the meeting—because Camille wouldn't let it go—was that we all knew how to play the song "Tequila" from memory. That's the song we played while the cheerleaders danced during halftime at home basketball games during the year. We decided we'd play that at our Spunk River concert, but we didn't practice because like six of us had to be home by ten and Austin and Tess were getting bitten by mosquitoes on the deck. The party broke up.

I loved it. I had a great time. My leadership bone was getting strong, right?

Yeah, Camille was pissed at me. She had a right to be pissed too. I wasn't being very nice to her. I didn't respect the concert. I butted into her speech. She was unhappy, sir. Camille was dealing with pretty complicated emotions too. She left when everyone else did. Right before she went out the door, she whispered, "Justin and Janessa."

"Oh, shit," I said. "You know."

"You and RC III. What am I supposed to do?"

"I don't know," I said.

"Me either," she said.

"I'm not dating RC III," I said.

"This is the worst summer ever," she said. Then she left.

What could I do? I stayed behind and helped Gore clean up.

Gore put some dance music on. Like drum machine synthesizer euro club crap that I wouldn't normally like, except Gore danced around cleaning. She danced all over the place, shaking her big booty. It was awesome, man.

Sure, I did a little ass-shaking myself. You know I'm down to do so, given the right situation.

While we cleaned (picked up napkins and lemonade cups, loaded dishes into a dishwasher that looked more like a luxury airplane), Gore shouted, "You should be nicer to your girlfriend."

"Who?" I shouted back.

"Camille."

"Seriously. She's really not my girlfriend. Okay?"

"Nicer to your friend then," Gore said. "You shouldn't call the cheerleaders bitches either."

"Why not? Look at what they've done to us."

"You don't have to be like them. You're a nice boy, you know? You've always been nice to me."

"Not really."

"Polite at least, which made me like you because polite is so much better than most people in our grade."

"Our school is filled with idiots," I said. "That picture of me and Grandpa is proof."

"I think that picture is adorable," Gore said. Off she danced, bouncing up and down.

I felt a little warm. Gore has really pretty eyes and she can move really well, even though she's giant. And so I got a little tickle in my gut. I watched her and the tickle spread.

Then she said, "Where was RC III? Didn't he say he'd be here?"

That broke the spell, sir. "Oh. Yeah."

"Wonder why he didn't come."

"Um…texted right before I got here. Fight with his dad. Couldn't make it."

"Oh. That's sad. I like him a lot."

My heart slowed. "Yeah?" I said.

"Yeah. He's really cool, don't you think?"

"Could you give me a ride home?" I asked.

"Now?" Gore asked.

"I'm tired and it's past eleven. And I'm supposed to call if I'm going to be late and I didn't."

"All you poor people with your on-site parents," Gore said.

"My mom ran away to Japan," I said.

"That's cool," Gore said.

Then she drove me home.

Sure. I'll admit it flat out, sir. Despite everything— her murdering and her scary makeup—I found myself super attracted to Gore.

She didn't really murder, right?

No, Gore isn't anything like that big-boobed coach. I mean. I'm really attracted to Gore, not just, like, addicted to the…her…boobs? Jesus.

Okay. Let's talk about Kailey because that's easier.

I think part of the crack we're sold by the man is the whole notion of Kailey Kaus, you know? Her hair smells like lilacs because she puts expensive shit in her hair that smells like lilacs. It isn't like her hair grows from her head smelling like a spring morning. And she kicks around her legs like a sexy pony, and pretty soon, we're all convinced we love her because we love lush-haired, spring-smelling ponies because that's what the good life looks like on my computer, right? That's what the girls on advertising look like.

Gore isn't crack. She isn't just a powdered donut.

When she dropped me off, she grabbed my hand and said, "Thank you for letting me host your band. It was very fun."

I stared into her ghost eyes, which didn't blink, got lost for a second. "Uh-huh," I said. "Okay." I kept staring for a few seconds.

Then she tipped her head, looked past me, and said, "There are men watching us."

"What?"

"From your house," Gore said.

I turned to the house and saw Dad and Grandpa's heads in the picture window. "Bye," I said fast and got out.

It was kind of bad when I got inside.

Grandpa and Dad didn't know where I was and it was past my curfew. And they were jacked up. Dad's face was all red and his hands were trembling. I'm sure that's what got to Grandpa because he isn't so whacked out usually.

They glared at me, shook their heads, blocked my path to the hall and stairs.

"Hello?" I said.

"We're having a heart attack because we think you're dead, and meanwhile, you're out there in some car, sucking face with a zombie?" Grandpa shouted.

"We weren't sucking face," I said. "She just dropped me off."

"What the hell were you doing?" Dad shouted. "Where've you been?"

"Hanging out," I said. "I'm like twenty minutes late. What's the big deal?"

"What happened to that loud hippie girl?" Grandpa shouted. Then he smiled. "You find yourself a hotter number?"

"What? No," I said.

"Use your damn phone if you're going to be late," Dad said. "Or you're not going out at night. Do you understand?"

"Twenty minutes late," I said.

"You giving us lip?" Grandpa asked.

"No."

"You want me to ground you right now?" Dad asked.

"Are you kidding?"

"Don't push me," Dad said.

"Jesus Christ!" I shouted. "Fine. Sorry. I'm going to bed."

"That's lip!" Grandpa shouted.

I pushed past them and went downstairs fast.

Dad stood at the top and shouted after me, "You watch it, buddy. You watch it!"

Watch what? Man! Weird as hell. Dad stayed home from work to spy on me and then freaked out about twenty minutes? Clearly, something wasn't right with him. Isn't right.

He wasn't exactly pissed this morning, no. More like a zombie. He half-hugged me and told me he wanted to take me home. I was glad he couldn't take me home, to tell you the truth. I'd rather be here with you.

Anyway, I was pissed and I decided to write nasty things about the cheerleaders on Facebook. Stuff about them being strippers. *DANCE SQUAD ACTUALLY HIGHLY TRAINED TEENAGED HUMPING MACHINE.* Something like that. But when I opened Facebook, I saw the message from Mr. Shaver.

Barry Shaver, June 12 at 10:22 p.m.

Hey, all. I appreciate the notes of support. I made an awful mistake on top of my original, more terrible mistake. I didn't fight for you guys. I didn't fight for our band. Then I doubled up on my cowardice. This meeting with administration Friday might not go well. But you guys have to hang together. You'll still be the Minnekota Lake Area High School Band, our band, whether I'm with you or not. Keep working for one another. You're all great. I'm so sorry I let you all down.

How'd it make me feel?

Like I was sinking in mud. So sad. I love Shaver.

There were a ton of messages of support. I read through all of them. I left a message myself. It's in there someplace. I just said we'd always love him no matter what.

Yeah. Sure. Shaver made it easy for the school board to claim he incited the trouble. "Keep working for one another." He didn't do it though. We planned the protest before he wrote that message.

No, I didn't write anything about the stripper team. I went to sleep.

Do you have any ibuprofen on you? My scrapes are throbbing.

CHAPTER 18

Gore wasn't at the shop in the morning. Neither was RC III. Thursdays are the quietest days because the resort cabins turn over. Lots of people head home after their week on the lake. We were staffed low and expected a slow day. (Thankfully, it rained pretty bad too, which reinforces slower business.)

It was just me and Dante and he had the news station on the radio. I couldn't stop singing *Love, love will tear us apart...again,* which is a very, very good song that Gore played on her computer while we were all out there on her dock and I'll tell you this, sir: Dante just stood back and put his hands on his hips and said, "What in the hell happened to you, Chunky boy?"

"What?" I asked.

"What are you singing about? You don't sing."

"I have songs stuck in my head all the time."

"But you don't sing. I'm telling you, kid. I've heard

you shout a lot and make a bunch of fart noises, but I've never heard you sing. What in the hell happened?"

"Make the donuts, dude," I said. But I smiled. And I kept singing. I was thinking about Gore for sure. I sang and sang.

Well, it was a stupid day otherwise, so why not dwell on my singing for a little, right, Mr. Rodriguez? Better laugh than cry. In this case anyway.

Apparently, I'm the only one who thought it was a bad day. I still think we failed.

Enough customers to make time move. A song in my heart. The morning cruised past. Then it was time for my very first protest.

Camille picked me up from work. She would barely talk to me in the car really. She has problems, you know? I mean, she's not the only person in the world. Selfish.

We got up to the school and there were a bunch of cars in the lot already.

It was a good turnout, sir. You know that. Cops have a pretty good list of names.

Fifteen band members showed up, plus Gore. (We gained a couple people in the crew overnight because of Shaver's message, I'm sure.) We all gathered in front of the doors and I said, "Remember, totally silent. Don't say a word to anyone. We're just going to go in there and we're going to freak them out with our silence. I'll write a note letting them know that it's only going to get worse and worse unless they leave Shaver alone and bring back band camp." (I held up a notebook, which I should've written in before going into the school.)

Maybe Austin Bates is smarter than he seems because while everybody else nodded like the plan was genius, he said, "Worse how, yo? Like, as in more fat asses and dipshits gonna stand there in a crew staring into space for no apparent reason. How is that scary?"

Schae Petersen said, "This is called nonviolent protest, Austin. Like Martin Luther King Jr. and Gandhi."

"Gandhi?" Austin asked. "That like chronic, girl?"

"I fear for our future," Camille said.

"Let's go," I said.

The school door was open. We entered the building. The gym doors were closed. I could hear Ms. Clark, the big-boobed blond lady, barking her dance team orders. "Get crispy on it, ladies. Turn. Squat. Explode!"

Tess and Austin giggled. (I assume about squat and explode.) I glared at them. And then—

Right, sir, I'm not proud. I don't care what anyone says. This was embarrassing.

We stood there for five minutes and did nothing but breathe and shrug and clear our throats until RC III walked out of the locker room with Joe Wruck. RC III stopped in his tracks and stared at us, and we all stared back at him. And then he laughed and said, "Gabe, man, what in the world are you doing?"

I shook my head because we made the silence pact.

He smiled. "You all look foolish, you know?"

"Hell yeah, we do. This is shit!" Austin shouted. "Why we following this fat-ass speedo underpants butternuts with this bullshit, Tess? Come on, girl." Austin walked up to the gym doors and pounded on them. "Woo! Y'all are whores! All of yuh!"

RC III took a step forward. His smile was gone. "Dude. Leave…now."

Austin froze. "Me?"

"You," RC III replied.

"Fine." He turned and left fast. Tess sort of stepped toward the door, turned back to look at us, and then ran after him.

Then, of course, because Austin had made a ruckus,

Big Boobs bounded out the gym door and screamed, "Who shouted that? Who are you? You'd better fess up right now or I'll get all of you."

Then Deevers came bounding down the hall from his office. "What are you kids doing in here? What are you—Who—Chunk? What are you doing?"

Again, sir, I didn't say anything because we'd made the damn silence pact. I should've been writing in the notebook, giving him our demands, but I was frozen on a stick, scared shitless, ice balls in my veins.

"You're not allowed in the building without supervision, guys. Okay? Okay? Get out right now. Right this minute," Deevers said. His face turned dark red. He looked like he was going to get sick.

We followed his orders. We did. We all shuffled to the exit, our silence pact intact. I was trembling with fear. I didn't write a damn thing in that notebook.

If I'm being honest, sir, I didn't know at the time exactly what our goal was other than doing something, to not just accept the crap.

Like I said, nobody else thought it was stupid. (They might have thought it was stupid if Austin hadn't pounded on the door to give us a little attention.) Everybody gathered in the parking lot and high-fived and talked about how Deevers turned red and how Big Boobs screamed. I think just getting yelled at was enough of an adrenaline charge to make most of us think we'd done something big. This was not a crew of people who had gotten yelled at much in their lives. (As class clown, I was more used to the yelling, I guess.)

I was a little depressed. Maybe embarrassed. I thought about RC III, who was still inside. Then I remembered Austin calling me butternuts and I got pissed, felt victimized.

"Wait," I shouted. "What are you guys so happy about? Do you realize we just got pushed out of our own school for no reason? We weren't doing anything but standing there. How is that a crime? How does that merit removal? Those football players just get to hang out in the building. The school treats us like we don't belong."

Everyone fell silent and stared at me. The sun beat down on my head, reflected off the shiny cars all around me. It burned my eyes.

Then Camille said, "Who in the heck does that

blond woman think she is? Why should she have any power over us?"

Austin Bates said, "Deevers is a bitch, y'all. I'm sick of it."

Schae Petersen said, "Did you hear him say 'Okay? Okay?' like that? He's a douche!"

Then Gore pretty much reiterated what I said. "Why do we get treated like criminals? We didn't do anything. I don't do anything wrong. We were just standing there. The cheerleaders can dance and shout and that's great. But we can't even stand quietly in our own school?"

I sat back on the front of Gore's station wagon. I nodded at these people. I said, "If we're going to get treated like criminals for no reason, I think maybe we should act more like criminals. Think about it. Let's meet later. I have to go home."

Seriously, sir. I had to go home. I was so, so, so hungry. I wanted to stuff my face in private or I wanted to work out to stop myself from stuffing my face. The stress of the day took a toll on me. Stress makes a hole in me that needs filling.

CHAPTER 19

The hole.

Hunger like that is an attempt to fill up a hole, okay? It's pretty literal, sir. I feel like I have this hole, this empty space, that can't ever get filled up, and when I don't feel right, that hole is the only thing I can think about. It's begging to get filled, like it has a voice and a mind, and the voice keeps screaming for my attention until I fill that hole with a thousand pounds of food.

Gore drove me home and it seemed like maybe she wanted to hang out longer to talk or something. But I had this emptiness to deal with. "Gotta go," I said.

"Oh, okay," Gore said. "Um…bye."

My real self, my Gabe self (as opposed to my Chunk self), wanted to spend the rest of the day with Gore. My Chunk self needed attention real bad. "We'll talk later? Let's talk later, okay?"

"Yeah. That'd be nice," she said.

Then I went inside the house and opened the refrigerator. I thought, *Eat everything in the world.* Grandpa came into the kitchen and said, "Look who's back home staring at the cheese."

I looked back in the fridge at a block of cheeses that seemed ready to get stuck in my mouth. Then I blinked, slammed the fridge door, and then said, "Thanks for never leaving the house, Grandpa."

"What?"

"I'm just glad you're here. Let's work out."

We jumped rope downstairs for a damn hour. It was killer. By the end, I wanted to puke. But also, I didn't want to plow food in my face after that. Killing yourself with a jump rope takes away hunger, fills that damn hole, man. It really does. That's good to remember.

At dinner, Grandpa and I ate a big salad (gross) with plenty of dressing and some grilled chicken strips (not too shabby). Dad complained about the salad. "I'm not a rabbit. I'm a man." He took the chicken and made a bunch of chicken and cheese burritos. He prepared his burritos, ate his burritos, and left the table while Grandpa and I were still eating. Lettuce makes you eat slower, I swear to God. When Dad huffed and lumbered away from the table, Grandpa asked, "You sure you don't want to let him in on the program, Chunk? He's in terrible—I worry about the guy."

"Absolutely not," I said. "I don't want him to have a piece of this because I like this and he'll kill it."

Grandpa nodded. "Could be."

Grandpa knows Dad pretty well, right?

After dinner, I totally passed out on the couch. That was a big day. I led a totally ridiculous protest that did nothing but get us thrown out of school. But still, I *led* it and it *did* announce to Deevers and Big Boobs that we band members cared about what was happening to us. That's something.

Anyway, I passed out in front of the TV and I might've slept through until morning, except around quarter to nine, the doorbell rang.

Wait. Wait a second.

RC III isn't going to get in trouble because I'm telling you this, is he? He didn't do anything himself, just gave me some ideas.

Good. Okay. It was RC III. Grandpa shook me

awake. He said, "The quarterback is at the door. He doesn't want to come inside. Just wants to talk to you."

"Huh?" I asked. "What quarterback?"

"The black kid."

I rolled off the couch. Dad asked "Who?" from his recliner. I didn't answer, just headed for the door, slid on my flip-flops, and walked out.

"Hey?" I said to RC III. He stood in the front yard, his hoodie pulled up. I was a little embarrassed. Our house is pretty run down—a 1970s ranch-style shit pile with peeling paint. I bounced down off the stoop to make sure he didn't try to come in.

"Yeah. Hey," he said.

"What's up?" Felt very weird to have RC III in my yard.

"I don't know," he said. "I'm bored, man. Want to take a walk?"

"Uh…okay?" I said.

He turned and walked out to the street. There are no sidewalks in my part of town. Almost looks like a campground at night. Not too many streetlights, just lights from houses (with a bunch of lake flies buzzing in them everywhere you look). It was dark out there.

"What's going on?" I asked after we got a house or so away from mine.

"My pops thinks I should stay out of this. He thinks it's not my business. Why should I care about a gang of white kids who can't play band or whatever?"

"I don't know," I said. "Why should you care?"

"I don't know, except I like you a lot better than I like the football dudes who all think they're God's gift to this town."

"They do suck for the most part," I said.

"But I really don't know why I care," he said.

"Oh."

"But I do."

"Cool?"

"Okay. So you know about the Green Lake thing?" he asked.

"Sort of," I said. "I know there were those two murders last year."

"Yeah, man. Pops is representing this Native American dude against a whole town that's coming after him because he's an easy target, even though they don't have any hard evidence. He's the dude who always got drunk down at the bar. He's the dude who got in fights all the time, shouting names at people on the street. What jury of white people wouldn't figure he's worthless and guilty and deserves to get punished even if he didn't actually do the crime he's got pinned on him?"

"Uh-huh," I said. We walked about ten more steps. "I don't know what that guy has to do with us," I said.

"What you all are dealing with isn't going to put you in jail, I know, but it's kind of the same thing, man. You fools are such easy targets. Pull out that Justin Cornell kid and who you got left to defend you? That fake-ass gangster Austin boy? Easiest thing in the world is to take a fool's stuff."

"That's kind of offensive," I said.

"Sorry," RC III said.

"No problem," I said.

"Anyway, Pops says it's not my battle. But how is some Indian his battle?"

"I don't know."

RC III nodded. We walked a few more steps. "Can I tell you how to fight better?" RC III asked.

"Uh…sure," I said.

"First, man, you can't just stand out there in the

cafeteria like you're pigs waiting to get slaughtered. You have to do something."

"Seemed like a good idea at the time, okay? We were showing Deevers that he silenced us," I said. "With our silence."

"No. You have to make noise, get in the way, make some demands, tell Deevers and the cheerleaders what's going to happen if your demands don't get met."

"But we don't even have demands really. We're just mad."

"You demand fairness, man! Demand real democracy."

"I wrote about that in my letter to the editor."

"Yeah. It's a public school, man. You demand a hearing before things you care about get taken away. Demand a voice by lifting your voice. Make it hard for those cheerleaders to practice until you're heard."

"How?"

"Why didn't you have your instruments with you today?"

I stopped walking. "Because! Silence was the point!"

"You've been talking all week about having a

concert. That's where you should have your concert. What if you brought your instruments with you?"

"Oh, shit," I said. I thought. I dropped down and sat in the grass in front of the McDermotts' house. I thought some more. "Oh, yeah."

RC III dropped down and sat cross-legged on the grass next to me. "They didn't silence you. They didn't take the instruments. They're taking your education and your opportunities."

"Yeah," I said. "Yeah."

"I know from basketball how loud you can be with those damn horns and drums. I could hear you blasting on them through whole games during the season."

"Pep band is loud," I said.

"So don't stand out in the cafeteria quietly. Don't stand where the cheerleaders aren't."

"Should we just march into their practice?"

RC III thought for a moment. "How about this? Get up in the weight room above the gym. Bring your instruments. Blast those things. Stop their practice. Get Deevers in there. Tell him and the cheerleaders that you won't quit messing with them until somebody listens to you about the money and your education."

"Oh, yeah," I said. "But wait. How do we get up to the weight room? We can't go through the locker room and the coaches' offices. Isn't the outside entrance locked?"

"I work at Dante's in the morning. After work, if you've got the people, I'm going to let you in there. Coach Nelson gave me an outside key for when I can't go during regular hours."

"Dude, you could totally get in trouble."

"I'm going to let you in and leave. Don't tell anyone how you got in there. Maybe the door wasn't locked? Rest of the football team is running winds on the sand at Wilson Beach tomorrow. Nobody will see me."

"Okay," I said.

"Can you get your friends back there after what happened today?" he asked.

"Yeah. They thought today was a big success," I said.

RC III smiled huge and giggled. "You people are crazy. That was one pathetic display, man."

Just then, Mrs. McDermott leaned out her front door and screamed all crazy, "You boys get off my lawn. This isn't a park!"

"Sorry," I said. I stood up.

"What's her deal?" RC III whispered, eyeballing her. Mrs. McDermott glared at us from her open door. "She have something against black people?"

"She's been screaming at me to get off her lawn for ten years," I said. "She has something against people generally."

"Dude, I get that," RC III smiled.

He stood too and we walked back toward my house. We walked in silence for a few seconds. Then RC III cleared his throat.

"Yeah?" I asked

"Um," RC III said.

"What?"

"Are you into Chandra?"

I sort of stumbled, "Who?"

"Gore," RC III said.

"Well," I said. My chest got tight. "Probably." Then my head barked at me: *Shit! Don't say that!*

"She's pretty fine," he nodded.

"I don't know. Whatever. I've got other stuff. I've got some business to handle and I don't really have time to, you know, get all into sex."

"What, dude?" RC III laughed.

"Shit," I said. "Love."

"I wasn't asking you to marry her. I just noticed she talks about you all the time at work."

"She does?"

"Definitely, dude."

"Oh." Mr. Rodriguez, my heart sprang out of my chest, man. I...I...why the hell am I telling you this? Anyway, suddenly, I thought it was a really good idea to go to Gore's house. "Hey," I said. "I have to plan this protest thing for tomorrow because Shaver's hearing is tomorrow night, so I need to get on it. Maybe we should go over there. Go over to Gore's. Get Gore's help on it. I'd better call Camille. She's...she's a pain in my ass—" My voice sort of trailed off.

"You okay?" RC III asked.

"I think so," I said.

"I'll drop you off at Gore's if you want, but I have to get home. Pops hits the damn roof if I'm later than ten."

"Okay," I said. "Give me a ride!"

We got into his car and I didn't even think for a second about my own dad. RC III drove me to Gore's.

I texted Camille on the way. A couple minutes later, RC III dropped me off in Gore's front yard. As I got out of the car, he said, "We'll go do this protest after work tomorrow. Tell everybody 2:15."

"You got it," I said. "Thanks."

"Uh-huh."

I watched RC III turn the car around and peel away.

Yeah, he did let us in the school the next day, sir, but he had no other involvement in anything that happened.

I am telling the truth.

CHAPTER 20

I sat down in Gore's dark yard. I sort of couldn't believe I was there, sir. Why the hell was I there? Some slight information that Gore talked about me at work? I thought, *Oh, my God. You idiot.* My mouth got dry and I got all shaky and nervous.

It isn't too far a walk to home from Gore's. I could've done it. I thought about doing it. I stared out at the street and thought, *Hoof it home, dude.* But I'd texted Camille from RC III's car that we needed a planning session so…

So I sat down in the grass and waited for Camille to respond to my text about planning. Maybe she could pick me up and drive me home because I'd clearly gone off half-cocked in love. Or maybe I could knock on Gore's door more easily if Camille were with me. I stared at a streetlight down the block.

My phone buzzed in my pocket. *Thank God!*

But it wasn't Camille. It was Justin Cornell. He wrote this long text, something like:

Chunk, Seth Sellers is going to kick your ass if you do anything to mess with Emily. He told me to warn you. He's pissed that you aren't showing his girl respect. Or all the girls. Why would you go up to their practice two days in a row? Please take this seriously. I don't want anything happening to you, even though I'm pissed that you're such a jerk to me.

Me? I'm a jerk to Justin? How is that possible? How could he say that? He's hanging out with those guys and not calling me ever and I'm the jerk? If there's one person in my whole life who has done his best to remove my basic human dignity, it's Seth Sellers. Fart sounds? Making me ass-dance? Just the day before, he posted that picture of me and my grandpa in our shiny swimsuits. And Justin wants me to be afraid? What is Seth going to do? Kill me? He's already done his best to crush my freaking soul. I stood up from the grass. I thought, *Stick it in your ass, Cornell.* I thought, *Come and get me, Sellers.* I walked across the yard and rang the church bell doorbell. Gore answered. "Hi!" she said. "Where'd you come from?"

"The yard."

"Oh, yeah?"

"You have any lemonade?" I asked.

"Of course I do! Come on in!" she said.

We watched Adult Swim cartoons for a couple hours. We drank some lemonade. We sat really close to each other on the couch, which was pretty great. I could feel this amazing warmth coming off her arm.

I lost all fear, man. I was so mad about Justin.

Around 11:30, Gore turned to me and asked really quiet, "So did you just come over for lemonade?"

I swallowed hard, shook my head, and said, "No, we're going to have a real protest tomorrow. A big one."

"Really? There aren't any announcements on Facebook."

I thought for a second. "I'm not just going to post on Facebook. The cheer girls will see it. They're upset about what we're doing."

"Oh. That's good."

"Can I use your laptop? I need to send some messages."

"This is very exciting," she said, betraying absolutely no excitement in her voice.

"Yes," I said. "Very."

She exhaled. "Two weeks ago, nobody in the world liked me," she said.

"Two weeks ago, I was a stupid beach ball."

Gore reached over and put her hand on my hand. We locked eyes. She swallowed hard. I breathed in deep. I could drink her, you know? It felt like I was sucking helium, like I might start floating.

"I'll get my laptop," she said.

She let go of my hand, stood up, and skipped across the room and brought back her computer. She looked so pretty skipping.

Then I thought about stupid Justin Cornell.

Instead of posting in a public way, I made a list of everybody who had been to our silent but deadly protest earlier in the day. I logged into my Facebook and sent a message to as many of them as I could.

Go ahead, you already have my account open.

Gabe Johnson, June 13 at 11:44 p.m.

Tomorrow is the day, you Geekers. Tomorrow, the school board at an unannounced time and in an unannounced location will decide whether they should fire Mr. Shaver. We can't control what they do, but we can make it known that our dignity won't be taken from us, that we will have a voice. It's their choice whether our voice is creative or destructive. In either case, we will be heard! Geekers! Meet in the school parking lot at 2:15! Bring your instruments! We will have our concert in the weightlifting balcony! Those cheer girls will know that we are here! Spread this message to all who might feel as we do. Keep this message away from anyone who might want to stop us. We have already received threats from Major Asshole Jocks in the school. Until tomorrow, when we shall play our song!

I sent the message, and immediately, there were replies from Geeks getting cheeky about our power! They spread it everywhere.

Yes, sir, even to Randall Andersson, MLAHS band

alum and budding rock star. Hell yeah. He sent me a personal message. He said he'd try to get to the protest. Just wasn't sure their tour van would pull in early enough. Because of their Spunk River Days gig, the whole band spent the weekend at Randall's dad's cabin, I guess.

Take that Justin Cornell. Randall wants to hang with me, okay? Tell your great new pal Seth Sellers about that.

I maybe shouldn't be so hard on him. After last night anyway.

Yeah, I sent the message to Camille too. She didn't respond. I actually haven't seen her since our silent but deadly protest.

That's what I mean. A whole new set of friends, Mr. R.

A week earlier, there was Justin and Camille. In all honesty, both of them are decent people. Really good. But I want you to notice something because I did. Justin and Camille call me Chunk. RC III and Gore call me Gabe. That's my real name. My new friends give me proper respect, sir.

Gore likes to be called Gore or I would call her Chandra, I swear.

Here's where the problem with Dad got big. While I sent messages, Gore cooked us some veggie burgers. In the meantime, my phone went dead. Right after I ate, I fell asleep on one of those big leather couches. Gore covered me up in a blanket. Because her dad isn't around much, I don't think she even considered the possibility that I should go home. I didn't wake up until like 4:30 a.m., and by that time, I had to go to work. (Luckily, Gore had a Dante's T-shirt she never wore, and luckily, she's a big girl or I never would've fit in the thing.)

Why would you ask that? That's not an appropriate question, sir, okay? We held hands and she slept on the floor right beside the couch. I'm not some pervert who just wants to get lucky. Not now anyway. Gore is a woman. The real deal.

Apology accepted.

Sure. Maybe in the depths of my brain I was trying to make Dad mad or "assert my independence." He doesn't really care if I'm okay. He just wants to control me, like he wanted to control—Listen, the next morning, I was freaked about how Dad would react. It was an accident that I fell asleep. But I didn't want to deal—

Jesus. I'm really tired.

Yes! Jesus God, I'm tired of talking. Can I go back to the cell and go to bed?

What time? Tonight?

Why? Do you have a meeting or something about this whole deal? It's Sunday.

Okay, okay, okay. We'll go on.

I'm so tired.

CHAPTER 21

At 5:30, Gore drove me to work. We got there just as Dante was opening the back door. She leaned over and kissed me on the cheek right in front of him and his mouth dropped way open. I climbed out of Gore's car. Dante spread his arms out and he shouted, "Workplace romance! You're both fired! Didn't you read the small print in the contract?"

"Shut up, man," I said.

"Sure, Chunk. Whatever you say. I'll shut up about your romantic love life!"

He was way too delighted, Mr. R.

RC III got in a few minutes later. He didn't even really speak to me. Just got to loading different juices and milks into the drinks cooler out front. I think he was pretty nervous about what he'd agreed to do. He was sticking out his neck for us.

It was *not* a normal morning in a lot of ways. At

like nine o'clock, who should come into the store but Seth Sellers? I was serving some Twin Cities tourist lady when the front door bell rang. I felt this presence. I could tell someone was staring at me. After the lady paid, Seth was right in front of my face.

"Hey, donut boy, good to see you didn't eat up the whole stock."

My heart started pounding really hard. I could barely speak. "Ha-ha. Can I get you something?" I asked.

"What? Speak up."

I swallowed hard and then began to recover myself, began to get mad. "Do you want something?" I said louder.

"I want you to stop staring at Emily and Janessa, you fat pervert. Don't you dare come up to the school while they're practicing. Don't you show your fat face up there."

"Oh, really?" I said. "I can't go in my own school?"

"You heard me," he said.

Just then, RC III came out from in back. Seth shot up straight as a shovel handle, man. His face went totally red. "Hey," he nodded.

RC III just stared at him. Seth is a football player, so of course they know each other.

"I'm not going to get anything, I guess," Seth said. "Not that hungry. See you guys later." He winked at me, turned, and took off. The bell rang on the door as he exited.

I had to breathe hard to keep from falling over. Man, I'm not used to conflict like that. I'm used to ass-dancing and laughing it all away.

"What did he say to you?" RC III asked.

"Stay away from Janessa and Emily. Stay away from cheerleader practice."

RC III shook his head. "You should've let that fool have it, man. Kid's a waste of space."

"Yeah. Next time. Boom. Ha-ha," I said.

"Really, don't worry about him. I bet Emily likes the attention anyway, likes the drama of it all. That Janessa does for sure, man. Don't you worry about Seth Sellers."

I nodded. Then I thought I might throw up. But I didn't, so I count that as a victory.

No, I don't know, Mr. Rodriguez. I don't know if RC III knows Janessa and Emily at all. He…he talks to

Kailey. Talked to. I know he had a couple classes with her, but that wouldn't—He was just trying to make me feel better. Those girls did not enjoy the attention we gave them. I know that for a fact.

Okay. So that was weird. I'd never been verbally assaulted at work. But it wasn't anything compared to what was coming for me.

I was serving Vic Hansard, who owns the State Farm Insurance next door, when the real trouble came in the door. Grandpa and Dad.

Dad was as pale as Gore herself. Grandpa, on the other hand, turned blood red when he saw me doing my donut business as if nothing in the world had happened. As I rang Vic up, I saw them and gave a normal "Hey there!" kind of wave, which makes no sense—I mean, by that point, I knew for a fact Dad was going crazy. I'd plugged in my phone in back and I'd heard the messages. He'd left ten voice mails.

I don't know why I didn't call him back to tell him I was okay, that I'd just fallen asleep by accident.

Grandpa almost spat when I waved. "Well, he ain't dead in the lake," he said.

Dad just nodded and swallowed.

Vic turned to leave. He said, "Morning, gentlemen."

Grandpa replied "Yeeeeaahhh" in that gravelly voice of his.

The bell on the door rang, and the protection of Vic Hansard was gone.

There was no one else in the store because it was midmorning by then and the customers sort of dry up between early morning and noon. Thank God because Dad and Grandpa crowded right up to counter and they definitely would've frightened any customers who might've been in there. They scared RC III. He backed up against the wall, tilted his head down, and stared at the floor.

"What the hell are you doing?" Dad whispered. "Where in the hell have you been? Why are you here?"

"Uh…because I work here?"

"You never came home!" Dad shouted.

"It was an accident!" I said.

"Were you with him?" he pointed over at RC III, who pointed at himself and shook his head no.

Dante popped his head out from back, smiled, and said, "Hey there, Rob, why don't you come back here and help me lift some…lift some dough…onto the table?"

RC III nodded quick and disappeared in back.

"We'll talk later, okay?" I said fast. "You can't just shout in a business."

"Are you on drugs with that kid?" Grandpa whispered, jaw clenched.

"RC III? No! Are you serious? I wasn't with him at all! He drove me to Gore's."

"Who the hell is Gore? Is Gore that zombie chick's pimp?" Grandpa barked. Dante was clearly listening right at the door because he let out this big-ass laugh and then pretended he was coughing.

"Pimp?" I said. "Are you crazy?"

"Gabe," Dad whispered. "Where were you last night?"

"I'm sorry. It was stupid. I fell asleep at Chandra Wettlinger's house. She's Gore, the zombie you're referring to, and she's not a prostitute!"

Dante laughed loudly again, sir. Then he turned on the food processor, which drowned him out. Grandpa and Dad looked at the door and then back at me.

"I didn't sleep a wink," Dad hissed. "Your grandfather and I drove all over town. I called Justin, but he didn't know where you were, which scared me worse. I couldn't get the number of your quarterback friend. And I called and called you. Again and again, Gabe. You just had to pick up your damn phone, which I pay for exactly because I want to be able to get hold of you in circumstances like this."

"I'm so sorry, Dad," I said. "It went dead." I was breathless. Oh, shit, Mr. Rodriguez.

"You," Grandpa said, shaking his head.

"I'm sorry. I'm really sorry. I really didn't think you'd care," I said.

"Why the hell wouldn't he care if you're dead?" Grandpa hissed.

"I just didn't think you'd worry that much, Dad. You know I don't get in trouble like that."

"Come right home after work," Dad whispered. "I took the day off. We have some talking to do."

"Okay," I said. "Okay. Sorry."

"Good for you," Dad said. Then he turned and left.

Grandpa stood staring, his face still red, sort of trembling. "You're a fat turd. You got that? An ungrateful, fat turd," he said. That was like getting kicked square in the junk, sir. My stomach dropped.

"Jesus Christ, Grandpa," I whispered.

"See you at home, Chunk," he said.

Oh, crap. What a great morning, huh?

I just wanted to fold over and die, but it didn't end there, Mr. Rodriguez.

As soon as Grandpa and Dad left the store, RC III popped his head out from in back, blinked, then said to me (not Dante), "Sir, might Gabe and I take a quick break?"

"Ten minutes," Dante said. "Don't call Chandra's pimp! Ha-ha!"

I was shell shocked, you know? Wasn't exactly sure what was happening. Felt a little dizzy in my head, sir. I followed RC III around the counter and out the front door. He leapt up on the picnic table, pulled up his hood, which he wore underneath his donut T-shirt, and then said, "Man, that was one giant verbal ass-whupping you just got dealt."

"I had it coming," I mumbled. "But ow, my verbal ass hurts pretty bad now."

RC III took a deep breath. He nodded and then said, "You can't go home after work."

"No, I have to."

"You can't. You have a bigger responsibility."

I sat down in a plastic lawn chair next to the picnic table. "Dude, my dad might literally kill me, okay? I can't—"

"Hey, man. Have you noticed my name?" RC III asked.

I looked up at him, "Well, I clearly know your name."

"My pop's name is William. Bill."

"That's great," I said.

"But everybody calls me RC III like Robert Griffin the Third, right? RG III?"

"Uh-huh," I said.

"Dude. There's no Robert Carter the First. Pops is not Robert Carter Jr. He's Bill Carter. I'm RC III because RG III is a hero of mine. I named myself after RG III."

"Oh," I said. "I didn't know that."

"Nobody even thinks about it, except Pops, and I'll tell you this: It pisses him off. 'Your given name isn't grand enough for you?' He says shit like that."

"Oh?" I said because I didn't have a clue at what he was getting at. "Sorry?"

"No reason to be sorry. My pops is a hard ass and he gets on me all the time, grounds me for coming home one minute late. But I'm me. I'm RC III, man."

"Okay?"

"You gotta be Gabe. You set up this protest and Gabe has to be there, even if your old man kicks your ass for it."

"I can't," I whispered. "Dad's imbalanced."

"Don't talk to me about imbalanced. My pops took a thousand shots to the head playing ball. He's imbalanced. And you and me are supposed to be up at the school at 2:15, man."

"Dude, I can't."

"If you don't show today, your band nerd movement is done. You get that? It's all over. I'm not opening the school door without you, man. I can't be responsible for that without your leadership." RC III pushed himself off the tabletop, pulled down his hood. "We'd better go back in." RC III reentered the store.

I sat there, blinking. "Oh. Damn it. Okay," I said to an old lady with a dog who happened to be passing by.

When I reentered, Dante started making zombie prostitute jokes. But RC III told him "Not now" and Dante shut up. Wish I had that kind of power.

RC III didn't say another word to me. He didn't

even really look at me. He was friendly enough with customers. Many wanted to talk football with him. I think he was worried about the band nerd movement. He likes the band nerd movement. He likes me, I guess.

After the lunch rush, I pulled my phone off the charger, took a deep breath, shut my eyes, and called Dad. He answered right away. I said, "Dad, this is a lot to explain. But I'm leading a protest after work and I can't come home because everyone is counting on me."

"No," he said. "Come home."

"No, this is serious."

"Come home."

"I won't," I said. "You're…you're not listening to me."

"I'm telling you to come home."

"Sorry. Some things are too important."

"What the hell are you talking about? What kind of protest? Who do you have to protest?" he barked.

I hung up and felt like I'd been kicked in the wang because even though I don't really like my dad, I love my dad. I had to lock myself in the bathroom to regain my composure.

Yeah, he knew there was something going on with

the band! He's the one who told me to write the stupid letter to the editor!

Dad called back three times, but I didn't pick up. Then I texted his cell, This is important. I'm helping the band and all geeks.

Dad texted back, You'd better come home.

I didn't go home.

You know, when Mom first left, I stayed at Justin's for about a week. Dad couldn't feed me. He couldn't hold it together at all. He broke a bunch of Mom's stuff and he stayed up all night sort of trashing crap and crying, which was not too great for me to see. When I went to Justin's, Dad barely knew I was gone, I swear. Doesn't matter. It sucked. That time sucked bad. Anyway, one morning, me and Justin were watching *Adventure Time* in his basement, eating some pancakes, and during a commercial, Justin looked over at me and said, "My mom thinks your dad is emotionally controlling. He's, like, kind of abusive."

I looked at him, blinked, but didn't say anything because I was trying to figure out if what he was saying could possibly be true.

"Dude, you can totally live here if you need to. We want you to. Me, Mom, and Dad all agree," Justin said.

"Okay. Thanks," I said.

But right after I said thanks, I felt horrible, sir. That made me feel so bad for Dad. He's not a bad guy, Mr. Rodriguez. I think he's just had a crappy life. I don't think he was that bad to Mom and she was obviously not that nice to him, okay? I went back home the day Justin said that.

No, I don't want to hang out with Dad. Not at all.

No, no, definitely not. I don't blame him for being pissed at me about being at Gore's. I stayed out all night without telling him. Mom ran away without ever letting him know she'd fallen for some Japanese dude until she was already out the door. Makes sense he'd be freaked out.

Yeah. Yes, sir. Justin is a good guy. His parents are awesome and I miss them because they're my family too. They would've taken me in, no doubt. I'd probably be a far more successful human being if I'd lived with them instead of with Dad and old dirty-mouth Grandpa.

That makes me feel bad too. I really like my grandpa.

CHAPTER 22

We left right after the store closed. We didn't say a word while we rolled through Minnekota, but RC III smiled.

I wasn't smiling. I was nervous, had to shut off my phone. No more Dad texts.

RC III and I pulled into the parking lot in his Honda. There weren't many cars, but we were early by a few minutes. Gore was there. She sat on her hood with the Petersen twins. They were holding their French horns. I nodded at RC III and then climbed out and went over to her.

From there, we watched as RC III hoofed it to the west entrance of the school, where you can get into the weight room without going through the cafeteria.

"You think anyone's going to show?" I asked.

Schae Petersen nodded.

Gore said, "Yeah, according to the messages, maybe too many people."

"What do you mean?" I asked.

"Lots of Geekers out there," Schae said. Caitlin, her sister, smiled.

We fell into silence as RC III came back around the corner. He nodded to us, got into his car, and drove away.

Within a couple minutes, cars began flowing into the parking lot. Austin Bates's yellow Dodge Charger came roaring in. (I wasn't that pleased he'd come back after his dick-swinging moves the day before.) Then pickups, old shit Pontiacs, a Prius, a big-ass van (Mindy Solen's Dad's) filled with like eight people, and more. More and more.

And then the freaking tour van, okay? Wall of Sound rolled into the MLAHS parking lot. It took the van about thirty seconds to pull around. Everybody sort of swallowed their breath. Then all mouths hung open and they all looked like they'd been slapped in the face by the stupid stick. "Jesus, Mary, and Joseph," Schae whispered.

The bus came to a halt about thirty feet from

us. Then the door opened and Randall Andersson, MLAHS grad and band alum, climbed down. One other dude with curly black hair followed. He carried a bongo drum. Randall nodded and smiled at all the Geeks. Then he looked at me. "You Gabe Johnson?" Randall asked.

I nodded.

"Recognize you from Facebook."

"How are you?" I asked, sort of shaking in my shoes.

"Everybody else in the band is asleep, but me and Jake are in," he said. "We'll follow you, man."

I wanted to say, "Holy balls! Jesus! Holy nuts! What the hell are you doing here? I love you!" but I held it together. I said, "Cool." I felt the power, sir.

Then I looked around at the mass of people. "Okay," I said. "We're going to have to move fast. There's a ton of traffic out here. We're going to get recognized… stopped out here in the parking lot, right?"

Schae nodded. Gore nodded.

"It's time to roll. Get your instruments ready."

Gore, the Petersen girls, and I slid off the car and motioned at the others who were just pulling in to hurry it up.

I watched while Tess Cook pulled her clarinet out and started putting it together.

Then it dawned on me. "Oh, crap! My trombone!" I said. "I don't have it."

"No worries, Mr. Gabe. You're going to have to talk if there's talking to be done," Gore said.

"Just like middle school," Schae said. "Everyone is following you around."

I looked over at Schae and she was smiling hard just like smiley Caitlin, her twin. See, sir? I did have a natural leadership bone back in the day. It just went away for a couple years.

All around us, band geeks either held their instruments and stared at Randall or put together instruments without saying a word. Omar Fulwider and Cory Carlson pulled snare drums out of the back of Omar's car. Lots of people weren't band peeps at all actually.

Like small-sport jocks—cross-country runners and swimmers—and gamers and burners and chess players and crap. These people had brought kazoos and noisemakers like you use at New Year's parties. What a throng, man, all dressed for summer in shorts and

T-shirts and bikini tops (Tess). Didn't look like a 1960s protest from a movie—but pretty cool anyhow!

I looked at the office window behind the front hedges, Deevers's office. I could see a florescent light bank burning in there. No one looked out. When all instruments were assembled, I clapped a bunch of times. Everybody in the lot turned toward me. I motioned them to come closer. They all closed in.

"Here's the deal. The outside door to the balcony weight room is open. We're going to go in as quiet as damn mice, okay? We're going up the stairs and to the balcony, and then on cue, we're going to let those cheerleaders have it. We'll blow for a minute or two whether or not they're shouting at us. I'll cue you to stop. Then I'll say my piece. Everybody cool?"

Everyone nodded. Craig, Mark, and Teller, the cross-country guys, nodded. Jordan, Nick, Krissy, and Stephan, the gamers, nodded. All the many band people nodded. Randall and Jake from Wall of Sound nodded. Randall said, "Solid." Even the burners (and there were like ten dudes and Mike Timlin and Raj Weigel were smoking cigarettes) nodded. Only Austin Bates sat there smug. "Whatever, butternuts," he said.

"Don't screw this up, ass wipe," I spat back.

Gore grabbed my hand and smiled.

"Don't worry about me," Austin said, putting his hands over his head. "I'm cool, yo."

Man, that 90s rapper thing is irritating, sir. I didn't see him pull a huge Army duffel from his car before we went in. I turned and marched and thought everyone was right behind me.

RC III had done it. The door was open. We slid in without incident. Everybody really tiptoed because that back hall is all tile and concrete and it should've been noisy. I mean, it is noisy, but we all did great.

When we got to the top of the stairs, I pushed the weight room door open and poked my head in. There was no one in there, just like RC III had said. All football players were down running sand sprints at the beach. But I didn't hear anything from the gym either. From there, I should've heard the cheerleaders and their big-boobed, barky lady doing their thing. I looked back and held up my hand to tell no one to move and then I felt filled with adrenaline, my heart pounding in my throat so hard I worried someone could hear it, I got down on my hands and knees and crawled across the weight room floor—which is disgusting and sticky by the way—and slid up and peered over the edge of the balcony.

Sure enough, they were there. Kailey, Janessa, and Emily Yu were out front, drinking plastic bottles of water (not pop of course!) and Big Boobs was messing with the sound system in the corner.

A moment later, she clapped her hands like I had a few minutes earlier in the parking lot, got the girls' attention, and began barking instructions at them. *We need energy, girls! This isn't about turning on your little boyfriends. This is about showing the world that you're a force. The TV cameras are on you! What are you going to do about it?*

The dance squad lined up. Big Boobs pressed something on a remote. The music began to pound. And Kailey and the team got all speedy stripper on it.

I motioned for the hoard—there must've been forty of us in total—to follow me over to the balcony. Just natural as can be, they all slid across the floor, keeping their instruments from hitting up against one another or anything else. Dance music thudded. Nick, a gamer, had his phone out of his pocket. He held the phone up and took video. I also saw a couple other raised phones. We all nodded in time with the music. We all packed in by the balcony wall. Then I gestured with my fingers, heart exploding, 1, 2…3! And just like that, we all stood up and began blowing our horns and flutes and pounding our snares (and bongo) and screaming and whooping.

The cheerleaders stopped and stared, as did Big Boobs. We totally drowned out the stripper music. In a matter of moments, the band (even Randall Andersson's boy, Jake) naturally fell into playing the song we all know—"Tequila"!—like we do at basketball games and a couple of the younger cheerleaders started doing the "Tequila" dance from halftime. Big Boobs looked at us in shock, as did Kailey and Emily. But then Janessa started screaming (not that you could hear her) and the young cheerleaders (Jenny Case and Peri Jonas) stopped dancing. But we kept blowing hard and then Big Boobs took off running toward the main floor gym doors. And then Jenny and Peri, because obviously they couldn't help themselves, started dancing again. When it got to that part of the song, we all—including Jenny and Peri—shouted "Tequila!"

It was at this moment that Austin Bates did what he came to do, the bastard (maybe evil genius). He reached into his duffel and pulled out a giant water balloon. I saw it but didn't know how to react. In a split second, he and several burners began whipping giant water balloon after giant water balloon down onto the cheerleaders. They made direct hits on Kailey and Janessa and the splashes from the impact on the floor pretty well soaked everyone else. The burners kept throwing balloons until the cheerleaders began fleeing and then Austin and Tess ran down the back stairs to the gym floor and slid around in the water and whipped a couple balloons up at us.

Everybody laughed and screamed. Randall and Jake were totally cheering them on too.

Yes, sir. Gamer Nick got it all on video. Lots of people were taking pictures of the cheerleaders pressed against the walls too, not just Nick.

Then?

Then in came Deevers and Big Boobs. The stripper music was still playing. It sounded quiet compared to the noise we'd just made. Big Boobs clicked it off as they made it to the middle of the gym.

Most people were already running for the door. I stayed. So did Randall, Jake, and Gore. Austin and Tess bolted back out the side entrance of the gym and out of the building.

First thing Mr. Deevers said was, "Randall? What are you doing here?"

"I'm lodging an official complaint, Mr. Deevers."

"This isn't your business."

"You know it is. I'll be talking at you later, man." Then he turned to me. "Why don't you dudes join us up on stage for a song Sunday night?"

"Yeah. Okay. Cool," I said.

"Cool. Take it easy, Gabe," he said. Then he nodded and he and Jake, the bongo guy, left, leaving me and Gore alone with the aftermath.

I looked back down at Deevers and Big Boobs. Deevers's face was on fire, sir. His eyes were burning!

"Chunk. Get your ass down here right now."

I stood. I didn't say anything.

"Chunk. Down here."

"What about me?" Gore asked.

"I don't care about you," Deevers said.

"No, we're not coming down, Mr. Deevers. I'd like you to know that you are on notice. The cheerleaders are on notice. We know all about the pop machine."

Kailey looked down at the floor. She was soaked. Emily smiled and nodded slow.

"Duh. We posted signs about the pop machine, you idiot," Janessa shouted. Her hair was all sopping wet from the balloons.

"We know that not only did you take the money from the price hike, but you took all the money that accrued in that machine since the beginning of the semester. That's why our band camp was canceled. That's how you afford her!" I pointed at Big Boobs.

I assume I'm right about Big Boobs's pay.

I am? You know, Mr. Rodriguez? Good.

"Really?" Peri Jonas asked.

"Shut up," Janessa said.

"Furthermore, the way in which this whole deal went down shows a complete lack of respect for the band and for geeks in general, a lack of respect that, we suspect, borders on criminal—and we will pursue this, Mr. Deevers. We will not stop pursuing these actions until you have reversed course and put band program-ming back where it belongs."

"Chunk," Mr. Deevers said, all out of breath. "You're not supposed to be here. We don't have...

insurance. I don't know how you all got in without my noticing. But just get out. You're in over your head. This isn't your business. You're cruising for a bruising if you don't just—"

"You don't want Gabe to come down there?" Gore asked. "You wanted Gabe to come down a second ago. Why not now? What changed?"

Deevers looked visibly shaken, sir. I'm serious. He turned all kinds of colors and looked shaky. I felt… victory. Yeah, victory, for sure.

"We'll go. But we need to get our money back and we need to have summer marching rescheduled or else…we'll be back! We will disrupt again and again!" I shouted.

Then I turned and tore out of there. Gore followed right behind.

"Go, go, go!" I shouted.

"Geekers united!" Gore cried.

"Go Geekers!" I shouted.

The parking lot was emptying out. Cars were tearing out of there. It was amazing!

I don't know where Randall went after that. He didn't hang out with the Geekers. Pretty awesome he invited us on stage! Camille really should've been there. We got her concert. Maybe she'd be over there at Spunk River Days right now, getting ready, huh?

How the hell can I get on stage with Wall of Sound tonight? I'm incarcerated!

Yeah, of course I want to go to the concert.

I know. Too bad for me, huh? I'm a criminal. Shit.

No, Camille wasn't at the protest. She was AWOL. That's why I know for a fact that she's Baba Obi, the "I'm sorry" girl. I got all kinds of Facebook messages from Baba Obi. Camille was begging off.

I got maybe twenty messages in the last two days. Baba Obi? What a crazy-ass name, right? This Baba Obi doesn't have a single friend on Facebook, sir. She's not real. And that is a very Camille-sounding made-up name.

Baba? Like bah? Like a sheep? Camille's been obsessed with sheep since her dad bought a flock for their farm.

Oh, sure, yeah. Of course! Ha-ha. I did ask Camille if Baba Obi was her. I texted. I was all like, "What are you doing? Why all the apologies? Don't have to be sorry. Come on! We're pals! Just help me out. Help the Geekers!" She didn't respond.

She's a weird girl.

What did we do when we left the school? We ran! Gore hit that gas pedal and we flew out of the MLAHS parking lot. I turned on my phone. All these Geekers' texts poured in. Wilson Beach! they proclaimed. You coming, Gabe?

Hell yes, I texted back.

I don't know if there were messages from Dad. I turned the phone back off right away.

We got to the beach and it was awesome. People were flying high. I was actually psyched that Austin had brought those balloons. We high-fived. (Me and Austin? Crazy.) He said, "You and me make a good team, yo! Brains and the brawn!" I assume he was calling me the brains because he posed like my body-builder grandpa after he said it.

More Geekers gathered around me, everybody cheering and whooping, and I pretty much just told everybody, "We won it! We won that big and bad!" Then everybody went crazy and did all kinds of flips off the dock and people were swimming and dunking each other and making out. Band geeks and cross-country runners, burners and gamers. Theater dorks. Chess club freaks. Everybody started hooking up and it was just like the best ever!

Of course, this trip to the beach coincided with the end of the football dudes running wind sprints in the sand and also the beginning of the Spunk River Days festival. The music at the band shell doesn't start until 6 p.m. on Fridays. The carnival rides don't get going until about that time. But there are a lot of staff around and guess who's on the Minnekota City Parks staff?

Right.

Seth Sellers. Jason Wexler was there too. They were sweaty and gross—I assume from running the football sprints. They must've just finished running, but they had their Minnekota Parks shirts on. I'm sure all parks workers go on overtime during Spunk River Days.

I've thought a lot about this, sir. Seth did this to himself really. I wouldn't hurt a fly. I wouldn't hurt anyone.

I've always liked Jason Wexler too. Until the last couple days anyway.

While we were out there on the beach having a good time, Seth and Jason came roaring up in a little city golf cart. Seth let it roll to a stop and then jumped off the thing and ran up to me. Jason walked slowly behind. Seth was on fire, Mr. Rodriguez. "What did I tell you this morning, fat ass? What did I say?" he shouted, pointing in my face.

I was a little stunned by his sudden presence, okay? I wasn't exactly verbose. "What?" I said.

"Just got a message about your water balloons. I told you to stay the hell away from Emily. Stay away. And what do you do?" Then he shoved me hard, knocked me backward, and I fell on my ass.

"Don't, you jerk," Gore spat. She pushed him.

"Better back off, Chandra," Jason said.

"Screw off," Gore said.

"Just get away from me, freak," Seth said. "This isn't about you."

"Yes, it is," Gore said.

Then Seth shoved her and she almost fell down.

A gaggle of Geekers circled round.

"Jesus, Seth," Jason said. "She's a girl."

"She's a mutant," Seth spat.

"She is not," Schae shouted. She stepped toward Seth. "You're the mut—" Sir, Schae is small. He reared back and smacked Schae in the shoulders super hard, knocked her down, and that was it.

Yeah. It.

Austin Bates, Mike Timlin, Raj Weigel, Gore, Schae, they went nuts on him. Mike jumped him from behind. Austin and Raj punched him. Seth fell to the ground. Schae and Gore kicked him. Jason tried to stop it, but he seemed more scared than anything. He just kept saying, "Stop, guys. Stop!" I watched for a few seconds and then joined Jason, trying to stop it. Jason pulled Austin off. I pulled Mike and Raj off because they were hell-bent on killing Seth, it seemed like. I shouted, "Stop! Stop! He's a waste of space! Stop!" Crap like that. Jason and I managed to move everyone away from Seth.

Seth rolled over on the ground. His face was bloody. He pushed himself up fast.

"Don't you mess with the Geekers, yo. We'll hand you your damn ass every time," Austin said.

Seth spit a big wad of blood. He nodded. "It's on," he said.

"We'll see," Mike said.

Then Seth turned and walked slowly back to his golf cart. Jason followed like five steps behind him.

"We'd all better flee before the po-po arrives," Austin said.

Yeah, Mr. Rodriguez. That was definitely the Spunk River War going on right there.

CHAPTER 23

Gore and I took off for her house, which isn't far from Wilson. She parked in the garage and put down the door. We sat in the dark in her car, just staring straight forward.

"Did that really happen?" she asked.

"I think so," I said.

"I'm shaking," Gore said.

"Uh-huh."

We didn't say a word for a while longer, just breathed in the dark. Then Gore said, "I need something to drink."

A few minutes later, we sat in big wood Adirondack chairs by the lake, drinking lemonade. Again, sir, I said nothing. I didn't know what to say. I didn't know what Gore was thinking. She stared into the water. You know, I don't like Seth Sellers, but seeing him get the shit kicked out of him scared me. I didn't like that at all.

Twin Cities people on their wave runners buzzed by. Big, puffy clouds turned orange. Time must've passed, I guess, because soon we could hear some classic rock cover band blaring from the band shell at Spunk River Days.

I tried to make a joke. "I think that must be Camille and the nonprotesting faction of the MLAHS pep band. I didn't know she could play Steve Miller."

Gore's lower lip quivered. She teared up. "I still want to kill Seth Sellers," she said quietly. "I hate this."

"I know."

"I really am a murderer," Gore said. "I want to kill Seth Sellers."

"No, you don't," I said.

"I do. I hate him."

"It's okay—He—It's—"

"No, I've spent the last two years learning how to stay away from you people."

"You people?"

"People who call people bitches and sluts and jocks and…and psychos."

"I'm not one of—I'm not that person."

Gore shook her head. "I shouldn't let you call me Gore. I shouldn't let you be here. I should be alone."

"You want me to go?"

"Yes. No," Gore said. "Yes."

"I'll go. Okay. I'm sorry."

I sat there for a second longer, but Gore didn't say anything more. She stared at the water. I stood up. "Can I do anything?" I asked. "Can I call you Chandra?"

"No," she whispered.

"Okay," I said.

So I left. I lumbered around the side of the house and out to the street and started the walk home. I was so heavy, sir. I like Gore.

You know, I called cheerleaders "bitches" and jocks "jocks." And I'd called Gore a psycho in the past and I called her Gore, which wasn't meant to be nice. I'm a name-caller. I'm not sure what to make of it all yet.

No, I didn't go home. I only got a couple blocks away. I could hear the music echoing through the neighborhood.

The classic rock cover band over at Spunk River Days started playing this song that went something like *You're my angel! Never want to be alone! You're my angel and my home!* Or something like that. It's a really sad song. It's about love and being at home and not lonely, except the dude singing is definitely without the girl he loves. I stopped out there on the street and listened and the sky got that evening purple like Gore's eyes. And I was like, *No. Don't want to be alone. Screw it. No. I'm not going. You're my angel!* I turned around and ran back to Gore's house, ran through the side yard, back out onto their giant patio. Gore saw me. She stood up. I ran to her. It got all TV movie, like the kinds I watched with Mom when I was a kid. "I'm not leaving you," I said.

She nodded. "Thank you," she said.

I put my hands around her waist, leaned up to her.

We kissed. The seagulls flew and the sky got darker purple. The Spunk River noise faded out and it was just me and Gore kissing.

"Really. Thank you for not leaving me," she whispered.

"I won't leave you," I said.

Then the back door popped open. Then her dad came out to the deck! So did a bunch of other dudes!

Seriously. Out of nowhere, out walked five middle-aged men in Hawaiian shirts and flip-flops.

"Uh…hi?" I said.

"Dad!" Gore called.

"Chandra? Do you have a friend over? A boy? What's going on?" Mr. Wettlinger smiled big.

"This is Gabe."

"Yes, yes. Gabriel Johnson. I know you," he smiled.

"Hi. Hello, Mr. Wettlinger," I said. I thought I might have a heart attack. I had been kissing this man's zombie daughter.

Mr. Wettlinger carried two bottles of wine. The other guys were carrying food.

"Would you two like to join us for some barbecue?" Mr. Wettlinger asked.

Gore looked at me. Shrugged. She said, "We could use a little fun."

"Are you two okay?" asked Mr. Wettlinger.

Gore shrugged again.

"I think so," I said.

"I think we'd like to eat," Gore said.

"Burgers will be grilled!" he said.

An hour later all the dudes were barbecuing and swimming and me and Gore were having a great time, forgetting everything bad. We ate a bunch of chicken and cheeseburgers. (I had one cheeseburger and a piece of chicken.) The dudes said really funny things, which I can't repeat because they had potty mouths and I don't want any of that to be recorded, sir.

Then the dudes had that dance party I was telling you about during lunch. Man, did we dance. And Gore's such a good dancer! She has the best high-speed stripper moves ever! When Kailey's mom kicked Gore out of the dance school back in middle school, she made a huge mistake!

Yeah, that had a lot to do with Gore's death threats back in the day. What a loss to the stripper team at school! Gore would've been a superstar if she'd been allowed to participate in that!

I don't think I've ever danced disco, sir. But I'm a natural.

I did a lot of hip-bumping and finger-pointing. Gore kept spinning over and dipping me and then spinning away to do her stripper moves. I acted all unimpressed by her moves so I'd look cool dancing, but I was very, very impressed!

Oh. man, it was such a good time.

Until—Cue the buzzkill music please.

Your phone is buzzing again, Mr. Rodriguez.

CHAPTER 24

That was your wife? How is she? Do you like being married, Mr. Rodriguez?

I do want to get married. Definitely. I want to have kids too so I can be really nice to them and raise them right. I'd like to have a family band or orchestra or something. Gore could be a dancer because she doesn't play an instrument. Maybe I could teach her to play though.

Oh, yeah. Sorry. We were disco dancing with Mr. Wettlinger's pals.

Dad showed up.

I'd totally, 100 percent forgotten that he'd been in the shop that morning, that I'd stayed overnight at Gore's the night before, that he'd told me to come straight home after work, and that I'd totally stuck that crap right in his big, sad nose. I was wearing Gore's T-shirt still. I'd led a huge protest, been involved in a brawl, lost and found the woman I love, gotten involved in a dance-off on the lakeshore. I had forgotten Dad. Seemed like everything was going on at once.

He just appeared. He didn't ring the doorbell as far as I know. I looked over to my right at one point and there he was standing in Gore's backyard, watching me like a screwed-up, giant ghost that had arrived out of thin air. His shirt was untucked and his hair was all messy. Gore's dad saw him, and they shook hands and talked for a minute. Then Dad motioned for me to follow him. Gore stared at me, her mouth hanging open. I shrugged. Whispered "Bye." I think I also whispered "I love you," which is a little over the top, I guess. Then I followed Dad away.

No, it wasn't late. It was like 8:30, sir. Not even totally dark out.

In the car, he wouldn't look at me. I told him all about the protest and how I'd led it (in a lot of words, sir! I went on and on) and how Deevers had responded. I told him about how I might have a girlfriend and how things were getting better for me so fast.

Dad breathed deep and said, "Shaver was fired this afternoon."

I stared out the window into the growing dark.

"Oh, no," I said. "I forgot that was even happening. So much—"

"You're forgetting a lot."

"Well, there's a lot going on," I said, raising my voice.

Then Dad whispered, "Dancing with those men?"

"What?"

"You defy me and go dancing."

"Please, Dad. Please understand. This has been a crazy week, okay? Please?"

"Dancing," he said, shaking his head.

At our house, he pulled into the driveway, into the garage, then got out of the car. I got out too. Then he turned to me and said, "Give me your phone."

I stood staring at him, hating him.

"Give it to me now, Gabe. You've lost your privileges."

"Did you hear me? I have a lot going on right now."

"Now," Dad hissed.

"Fine," I said. I pulled my phone out of my pocket and put it on the floor next to me.

Dad glared hard. "Go in the house. New rules."

I walked into the dining room. Grandpa leaned over the stove, stirring a pot. He nodded at me. Real nervous. Not like Grandpa at all.

Dad followed me in a second later (I guess after he picked up my phone). "Sit down in the living room, Gabe," Dad said.

I took a breath and did what he told me to do. In the living room, I said, "Dad, please. I appreciate that you're upset and I get it. But you're not hearing me. This week has been—"

"Shut up," Dad said. "Shut your mouth. I've heard enough."

"I…just wait. Dad—"

"I said enough!" he screamed. He breathed hard. His eyes watered. "Here's how it's going to be. You're not to leave this house. You're not to talk to anyone. No computer. No phone. No landline. No job. No girlfriend. No nothing! Do you understand?"

"No job?"

"I've already talked to Dante. You're not to go in."

"Dad!"

"You will obey me. You will pay attention to what I say. You will not live under my roof and eat my food but treat me like I'm some minor annoyance you can swat away without thinking twice."

"Dad, I never—"

"You will do nothing!" Dad screamed. His chin began quivering. He let out a little cry, sir. I'm serious. Like the beginning of a sob. Then he turned and stomped away back to his room, where he slammed the door shut.

I looked over at Grandpa. "He took your computer," he said.

"What the hell am I supposed to do?" I shouted. "Dad!"

No answer.

Grandpa shook his head. "Boy," he whispered. "Tough times. Come here, Gabe. You want some spinach soup?"

"Shit," I whispered. "No," I said and I headed for my terrible doghouse.

Hey. "Did you know somebody egged our windows?" Grandpa called after me as I climbed down the stairs. "Ten minutes ago. Three boys. Let launch about a dozen before I chased them away. You know what that's about?"

I didn't answer.

What about Shaver, sir?

Yeah, school board. Met at Kaus's house, for God's

sake. With Mr. Deevers's consent, they dismissed Mr. Shaver not only for his drunk-driving ticket but because he had gotten on Facebook and incited a riot at the school. That "riot" had nothing to do with Shaver. He held no sway over us. The school board is just wrong. They know they're wrong. They don't care. They just like slapping us around.

Jesus. It's still all new, sir. This whole thing. Shaver's such a good guy. Why did he get drunk like that?

Yeah, we're not a band at all anymore.

Okay. I went a little crazy.

When you're used to being connected all the time and suddenly you can't get any word about anything that's going on and someone has egged your house and your band teacher has been fired and you've just gotten what seems to be your first legitimate girlfriend but you can't talk to her, you start to go crazy. At least, I did.

I lay down in my bed, tossed and turned, then showered because I smelled like a sweaty donut. Then I lay down in my bed again and started to sweat again, getting all twisted up in my sheets, and I cursed Dad's name because I felt a great hatred for him deep in my guts.

I started thinking about what he'd said. It wasn't "No work for a week." He'd said, "No work." For how long? Forever? Was crazy, terrible Dad cooping me up in the house forever? I'd be like some pale freak trembling in the corner of the basement when the police finally came for me?

Then I thought, *Oh, my God! We're being egged. Shit!* I knew exactly what that was about. Seth Sellers was coming after us! Shouldn't I call Gore to let her know? I needed to call her! Shouldn't I Facebook Austin Bates because Seth would be coming after him? And Mike Timlin and Raj? The jocks would beat those guys hard, right? Not just throw some eggs! I needed to do something. I couldn't do anything.

Just me and my thoughts, sir. Not a good combination.

The school board fired Mr. Shaver! They took our money, drove Shaver crazy, and then fired the guy!

Look who loses. Look at the loser. I'm the biggest loser in the world.

I'd only been down there for like forty-five minutes at that point, I swear. But I lost all hope, plowed into the swamp of despair, and the hole opened up.

Okay. For more than a week, I hadn't gone into the refrigerator, you know? In that week, I'd become the leader of a movement (a small and dumb-ass movement that was losing bad—but hey). In that week I'd gone from having friends who call me Chunk to hanging out with a great quarterback and a hot goth chick who respect me. I can't tell you how hard I'd worked, Mr. Rodriguez. I tried so hard and Dad was taking it all away. No Dante's meant no RC III, no Gore. Trapped again.

Yeah, trapped, sir. After Mom left, I went to Justin's for a week. When I came back home, I pretty much stayed with Dad all day long, all night long, all weekend long. It wasn't because Dad stopped me from going then. He never said that I couldn't leave and see friends, but he was so ripped up, okay? He just kept crying and I was scared. Mom told me to take care of him, so I didn't want to leave him alone. I'd pay the pizza guy at the door or walk over to the IGA to buy chips and cookies and crap. I called into the college a bunch of times to tell his secretary he was sick and I stayed home from school a bunch of times to keep an eye on him. On Saturdays, when I would normally be over at Justin's playing video games or whatever, I sat in front of the TV and I ate with him because I didn't know what to do, because I wanted him to be okay. And look what happened to me. Look what became of me.

Dad didn't want me to escape Chunk.

I did the wrong thing, Mr. R. I reacted badly.

I felt empty. I felt alone again. I thought, *Screw it. I'm going to fill this. I'm going to eat myself to death if I have to. You like that, Dad? You want me to be Chunk?*

Because I'd been so under control, I was weirdly excited to go after it. I got a burst of adrenaline.

I leapt back up the stairs from my sweaty bed and went into the cupboard, where there are usually chips. There weren't potato chips, just a half-eaten bag of tortilla chips, which didn't sound like it would hit the spot. If I was going Mexican, I wanted real tortillas. Grandpa stared at me from the table, a bowl of soup in front of him.

"Spinach soup?" he asked.

"No," I said. "We have tortillas?"

"Fridge," he said.

I went into the fridge and grabbed tortillas and shredded cheddar and sour cream and salsa and I assembled a bunch of cheese burritos on a platter.

"Gabe?" Grandpa asked.

"Mexican," I said.

I stuck them in the microwave for like thirty seconds. The cheese didn't even melt completely, but I was hungry. I whipped a bunch of sour cream on top and then headed to the table to eat. Grandpa took a deep, sad breath, got up, and went into the living room.

Oh, balls, Mr. R. I sucked those suckers down. Didn't even taste them. Inhaled the crap out of them. Then I was still hungry, but we were out of tortillas. I went back into the cupboard for the old tortilla chips, dumped them on a plate, dumped cheese on top, microwaved the pile, and ate the stack with salsa and the rest of the sour cream. Didn't taste a thing. Sucked the suckers down.

I needed more. So I opened the fridge again. Bread, ham, butter. I pulled them out of the middle shelf. I couldn't find Swiss cheese, which is what I like on my ham sandwiches. I bent down to look in the back of the fridge and saw it. Not Code Red but straight-up old-school Mountain Dew. Two 20-ounce bottles. "Holy shit," I whispered. "Shit."

Grandpa wouldn't buy that crap. Dad bought it. Dad doesn't drink Dew. He's a Coke guy. He bought it for me, Mr. R. He had to have bought it for me.

My dad doesn't know how to care for me. He was trying to be nice in the crappiest kid of way. I know it. That asshole! Fine, I thought. You got it.

I reached for a Dew. I pulled it out. I opened it. Took a swig. The liquid fizzed in the back of my throat. The sugar stung in my mouth. I took another swig and choked a little. Then I felt the real weight inside me. I'd eaten dinner at Gore's. I'd eaten six burritos. I'd eaten a giant plate of nachos. I'd kissed the enemy, the lip of the Dew. My stomach turned hard. I coughed, choked. "Oh, shit. Oh, no," I said. "Oh, shit!"

"You good, Gabe?" Grandpa called from the living room. "You okay?"

I coughed more, put the Dew on the counter, and stumbled downstairs.

In bed, my whole body ached and I could barely breathe. After an hour, I tried to throw up, but I couldn't. I sweated so much and my head pounded. I lay back down and tried to sleep.

Then around eleven, something weird happened.

I was buried in pillows, suffering huge nausea when the landline rang. Our landline almost never rings. Nobody knows the number. It's unlisted. It's only for emergency. In fact, because me, Dad, and Grandpa all have cell phones, I don't even know why we have it. Of my friends, only two knew the number.

Justin and Camille.

Grandpa answered and I pushed myself up in bed, strained my ears.

"No…no…he can't come to the phone. Grounded. No. No. I told you, no!" He hung up.

"Jesus Christ!" I shouted. There was silence, but I could tell Grandpa was at the top of the stairs, looking down. Then my guts totally turned on me. I went to the bathroom and threw up bad. While I did, a door slammed above. I stopped barfing and heard Grandpa yelling at Dad. Then the door slammed again.

They were fighting about me.

CHAPTER 25

It was 8:30 a.m. I guess this was yesterday, although it feels like a year ago.

I'd woken up because I heard Dad leave to open up the community college for Saturday classes. He didn't say a word to me, you know? Grandpa definitely told him I went on that eating freak-out and he didn't care. He didn't stop down to say anything about how I hurt his feelings by disobeying him or how he was worried about me getting hurt by staying out all night. He just left for the day.

I was awake, groggy. I brushed my teeth twice but still had a bad taste in my mouth. I still felt ill—but not like I was going to throw up. My heart beat funny, high in my chest, like it was trying to get out. I read a mystery novel Mom had in her collection (which I kept hidden in a box in the closet) to keep my mind off all the crap in the world. But I couldn't concentrate.

That's when someone started pounding on the front door. I sat up. I heard Grandpa talking to this someone. I even heard him say I wasn't available because I was grounded. Justin is good like that. He talked his way in.

I put down Mom's mystery novel and shakily climbed the stairs and met Justin in the hall off the kitchen. He was pale and trembling. So mad. His oxford wasn't buttoned right.

I whispered, "Oh. Jesus. What?"

"I didn't know you were capable of this, dude."

My heart accelerated. "I guess getting robbed by the school changes a guy," I said.

"You know this isn't about the band," he whispered.

"Of course it's about the band."

"No. It's about me. Something good happens to me and you want me to pay because I'm leaving you behind."

"Are you kidding? I'm leaving you behind," I said. "You have it backward."

"What are you talking about, Chunk?" he spat. "You're the same fat nerd."

"Go away, Justin. I don't have time for traitors."

"You have time for posting porn pics of my girl-friend though?"

"What are you talking about?"

"Don't play dumb, you fat freak!"

I took a deep breath, took a step forward so I was inches from him. "Say that again and you're dead," I said.

"Are you going to get Austin and Mike Timlin to kick my ass because you can't fight your own fights?"

"Dude, who are you?" I sneered at him.

"I'm the guy who's going to sue your ass for defamation of character. I'm the guy who's going to kick your ass for getting our teacher fired. I'm the guy you'd better not mess with ever again because it will get so ugly, Chunk, so bad for you. I'll teach you not to mess with our girlfriends."

I took a deep breath. Blinked. "Whose girlfriends?"

He paused for a second. He exhaled and then stood up straight. "Mine and Seth's."

I nodded at him. I took a deep breath, sir. "That's all I need to hear. Get out of my house."

"Chunk, you did this to me."

"No, dude. You're doing it to yourself, and if you ever call me Chunk again, you'll feel the weight of my foot on your skinny ass. Get out."

Justin's face turned the color of an apple, sir. He

looked like he was choking. "See you later," he whispered. He nodded, turned, and left.

I had to bend over to catch my breath. Man. That's the guy I almost lived with after my mom left me. His mom made cakes for me to make me feel better.

Okay, okay, okay—

Sir, my ass is killing me. Don't you pretty much know what happened after this? Haven't the police filled you in? I really, really feel like crap.

Fine. Okay.

Porn pics? Porn what? Of Janessa? How could I have anything to do with that? I couldn't begin to get my head around it, sir. I figured it was on the Internet someplace—but hey. No computer access.

After Justin left, without even thinking, I walked to the fridge, opened it up, looked in, and saw bread and cheese and ham. I saw the other bottle of Mountain Dew. *Shit.* I slammed the fridge and then went downstairs and started to sort of lose it, thinking about all the fun stuff Justin and I have done over the years, thinking about his mom and dad and singing stupid songs in the car with them while we rolled off on the family trips.

The Cornells took me with them. My mom and dad never took me anyplace.

I picked up the stupid mystery novel again, tried to stop thinking. Couldn't read it because my eyes were burning, so maybe I was crying.

That's when I heard footsteps on the stairs. I put the book down. A second later, Grandpa came around the corner.

"What do you want?" I whispered.

Grandpa sniffed, made a face. "You need to clean this place up. It's disgusting."

"Thanks. Thanks for creeping downstairs to insult me. I appreciate it."

"Aw, Gabe. Come on, kid."

"What?"

"I'm on your—I'm trying to help your ass out. That's my job. That's the only reason I'm in this sad little house of yours."

"Good work so far," I said.

"Hell yeah, good work. Got you exercising, didn't I?"

I took a deep breath, nodded. "Yeah. What do you want?"

"Okay. This is my assessment, boy. You ready?"

I shut my eyes, got ready for another insult, but that's not what came.

"Your dad isn't in good working order. I've been trying to tell him that you're acting like a regular teen-aged dumb ass, not a damn criminal, but he's not getting the message. I'm beginning to figure out that this jail cell he wants you locked in has more to do with your mother than it does you."

"I don't get it. How?" I asked.

"She'd been sneaking around for a year before he noticed, and by the time he noticed, she was already packing up her life to leave him for another man."

"I'm not his wife."

"He has no wife. He tried to get hold of your mother all afternoon yesterday to tell her about your troubles. When she finally responded to an email, she told him that you and he were a past life and she was no longer living in the same realm."

"What?" I gasped.

"She's gone, buddy. Gone nuts, if you ask me. But you're here and he went right to your zombie friend's place to find you after reading that message."

"What does Mom mean…realm?"

"I don't know, kid. But I'm sure somewhere at the bottom of your old man's injured heart, he thinks you're working hard to leave him behind too. And if you go, what's left for him?"

"I don't know. You?" I whispered.

"I ain't no prize."

"Different realm?"

I know lots of kids whose parents have gotten divorced, Mr. Rodriguez, but I'm the only kid I know whose mom divorced him too. I have a terrible mom. I collapsed back onto my bed.

Grandpa started talking fast. "Listen, Gabe. I can see it. I can see that you're climbing out of the shit river that you've been in since your idiot mom ran off. I hammer on you because I want you out of that river. And I'm real proud about…about the way you've been handling yourself of late. Working out. Arguing with that Cornell boy just now. Locking lips with a zombie. You have some fight in you."

I nodded, swallowed. "Thanks," I whispered. "Thanks for noticing."

"You can't stop just because your dad is still stuck in the river, okay? You have to keep showing that fight and you have to keep pulling on those weeds on that river-bank to pull yourself the whole way out. If that means telling your old man where to stick it and heading out of this house when he doesn't want you heading out, well…I want you to know you got my full blessing on that."

I pushed myself back up, looked at him. "Really?"

"I'll let you know if you're acting like an ass wipe, but I won't stop you from doing what's right."

"Okay. Okay," I whispered.

"You let me know how I can help you, Gabe. I'll help."

"I'm just going to lie here for a bit," I said.

Grandpa nodded. He turned to leave but then turned back around. "One more thing, buddy."

"Yeah?"

"Don't ever eat like that again. You scared me."

"I won't. I'm sorry."

You know, Mr. R., I always sort of hoped Mom would swoop back in and get me at some point. I always thought she was my way out of the mess. I didn't ever think it would be my grandpa.

I stayed downstairs for like an hour. Then I decided Grandpa was right.

CHAPTER 26

Every move I made from that moment on was deliberate and not crazy, Mr. Rodriguez. I got done feeling sorry for myself. I found Grandpa in the backyard, digging out dandelions. The morning sun was bright and strong! I said, "Who was that call from last night?"

Grandpa squinted up at me. "Hippy chick who flaps her arms when she talks."

"Camille."

He nodded. "She called to tell you your band is in trouble."

"Yeah, no kidding."

"And that her dad and her older brother had to chase kids in ski masks out of their garden. Vandals crushed tomato plants."

"Aw, Jesus. She wasn't even part of the protest." Adrenaline flowed in my veins. "I need my computer back, Grandpa."

"I don't know where it is, but your dumb mother's computer is in the closet in my room. Will that work?"

"Yes, sir. Thank you," I said. Then I marched in the house and into Grandpa's room and found Mom's old laptop on the top shelf of the closet. It was time for me to reengage with the world.

Your phone is buzzing, sir.

Go. Fine. I can sit in this room for the rest of my damn life. Just go ahead, Mr. Rodriguez. Answer your damn phone while I sit here forever.

Whatever. You just said "Yep" and hung up. Yep what? Come on!

If the phone call had something to do with me, will you please at least nod?

Is that a nod? That's a weak-ass nod, Mr. Rodriguez. Thanks a lot.

Computer.

I did start Geekers United, but I don't control everybody. Justin should've known I didn't have anything to do with that porn stuff. I'm no techie genius. Listen, sir, people get a little power and they use it, especially if they've been whacked with the shaft their whole crap lives, you know?

Gamer Nick apparently headed right home after

the protest and sliced and diced up his video of the cheerleaders and made a bunch of GIFs. He's pretty good with video.

The stripper one was great. Janessa, Kailey, and Emily out front grinding back and forth like they were aroused Barbies who were also really mad about something. Janessa's face is super funny in it because she's growling like a lion. Rwwawrrrrr!

Yeah, thus, the Janessa porn. Those computer dudes stuck her growling face on all kinds of gross Internet action. You imagine a gross thing a human being can do with a body and they stuck Janessa's head on that body. Pretty bad.

Nick made one GIF of Jenny Case and Peri Jonas, the "Tequila" dancing cheerleaders, dancing and then jumping really high when a water balloon smashed down. That was actually really cute, I thought.

There's a great GIF of me crawling across the floor toward the balcony too. *Captain Gabe sneaks to start the chaos!* I'm proud of that one because I look cool—like a spy—even though on the inside, I was a shivering mass of emotion, just scared. Nobody could see it on the outside.

Right. That's the classic. The most viewed. Slow-motion Kailey getting hit on the head by one of Austin's balloons and then seemingly screaming "Wooo!" while shaking the water out of her hair. Then she sticks out her butt.

It's dirty. I watched that one maybe a thousand times.

Yeah, her shirt goes sort of see-through and her eyes close. Her mouth opens, and when she spins her head around, it fires all this water into the air in an…in an erotic way.

Gamer Nick called it *Total Kaus-gasm*.

Geekers had a Tumblr that was filled with all these pictures and little animations and things. Don't mess with gamers, man. They'll get you.

Seth, Jason, Pete Erickson—they were the ones doing the vandalism, I think.

From Facebook, I found out that eggs were thrown at Gore's place and at the Petersen twins'. Camille's farm had plants smashed. Raj's car had the back window broken out of it.

Exactly. Worse.

Gamer Nick has a little sister and a little brother too. They were sitting there and watching Disney at 6 a.m.

Saturday when a freaking rock shattered the living room window.

Nick posted all kinds of pictures of the damage. He called the cops.

I'm sure it was Seth. He's the one who should be in jail.

I really, really doubt Justin was involved in any vandalism.

Why are you laughing about that?

Mr. Rodriguez, you're kind of weird.

In any case, Grandpa said I could leave, but I wasn't sure where to go. I didn't want to hunt down Seth by myself. Gore and RC III were at Dante's and I didn't want to go there because what if Dante called Dad?

I just looked at everything the Geekers were putting up. I laughed at the Janessa porn. I watched that Kailey video. I sent messages to people who were cleaning up egg vandalism and broken glass, telling them we'd figure out what to do about it all. I even wrote a note to Shaver to tell him I was sorry about what had happened.

Then I spent an hour writing a Kailey Kaus poem, which I sent over to Camille to try to cheer her up.

Yeah, a poem. It went with the Kaus-gasm GIF.

A nasty poem, not a love poem. Kailey Kaus is my enemy.

You don't believe me? Pull up my email. The poem's in the Sent folder. Sent it Saturday morning, man. Why would you question my distaste for that girl? Pull it up!

That big water balloon that crashes into her in the GIF was yellow, so I wrote the sun thing.

Kailey Cries…Kailey's Thighs

The sun is not the sun that brings fun.
It falls from the sky to dampen my boobs.
Makes me wet, upset, sunset of my soul.
Girls, my body wants to boogie but
My butt is soaked by geeks!
Is this my round bunny hump you seek?
Moist, no, drenched, a wench
Serving water to quench your nerd
Bellies full of hot dogs
And french fries and donuts?
Don't listen to my cries,

Hear the squeaking of my toned
Thighs. Because that is the true song
Of my one true heart—
(Whoopsies, a fart.)

That's a hell of a poem, man. And the way Kailey sticks out her butt in slow motion at the end totally looks like she's farting.

Get it, sir? I don't like Kailey Kaus.

Yes, I wrote an apology to the cheerleaders—but not because I like Kailey.

I just started to think a little more clearly about this stuff. Remember that Gore said she didn't like it when we called jocks "jocks"? Then around 10:30, I got a Facebook message from Ms. Feagan. She's so awesome. So great. You can pull that up too. It's in my messages.

Gabe, hi there—

I'm so sorry to hear what the school board did with Mr. Shaver. I already have a call into the union. What you guys are dealing with isn't right. I support you. I'm not the only one either. There are many, many adults in the community who are upset about the way the band has been treated the last couple weeks. Thanks to you and your crew of students for talking about it all over town yesterday. Nobody knew, but they know now. I'm very proud of you. That said, I'd like you to take a step back for a moment and think about who is and who isn't a legitimate target. The dirty pictures and videos your friends are posting cross the line. In the end, these girls are just doing what they're told. They're children just like you and they don't deserve to be punished the way you're punishing them. Remember when we talked about the notion of impermanence when we read *Thirteen Reasons Why*? Remember how you said that who we are at fifteen will change at sixteen, seventeen, twenty-five, thirty-five and is different from who we were at ten? I thought that was so smart, Gabe, so true. Janessa Rogers will be a different Janessa a year from now. Just like she was different when she was a little girl getting a hug from her grandmother. And in two hundred years, she'll be gone, nothing, probably no one will remember her at all. That's true of all of us, you know? Have some empathy for the Janessa that was and the Janessa who will be and the Janessa who will disappear one day, okay? If you're fighting, target the institutions, but don't target kids. Will you think about that for me please? Thanks, guy. I'm working for you, okay?

Ms. Feagan

Whoa, right?

Yeah, that was eye opening, Mr. R. I thought a lot about how I get treated and how nobody seems to care—or at least think about—how much I've already been through and how that shit can cut you. I figured we were doing to Janessa just what she'd done to me. We were robbing her of her dignity, right?

I sat there staring at Ms. Feagan's message for a couple minutes. Then I wrote her back and told her thanks and told her I'd do better—and I meant it.

That's why I sent personal apologies to every one of the cheerleaders, not because I like Kailey Kaus.

Only Janessa responded. She told me where to stick it, but that's cool. This fight isn't about her in the end.

After I sent those messages, Grandpa and I did a hellacious circuit workout. That's how I spent the rest of my morning. I didn't know what else to do. I even considered the possibility that this whole thing with the band was running its course and maybe Ms. Feagan and her friends would do the fighting moving forward. I breathed deep and got calm and even thought I might keep myself grounded, stay in the house for the day, try to talk to Dad about Mom and everything.

Then, during lunch, Grandpa turned on the radio. And there it was. KMLA's Dick Kolighter interviewing freaking Deevers and Chief Bartell live at Wilson Beach. They were talking about the great Spunk River War of 2014.

Can you believe how trumped up that crap is? There were two groups of teenagers who were pretty pissed at each other and that was it. War? Come on! It had nothing to do with Spunk River Days either.

"We've had multiple reports of vandalism and two reports of physical assaults," the chief said.

"This is related to the school having had to fire Barry Shaver," Deevers said. "The band kids aren't taking it well, but there's not a lot we can do. Mr. Shaver has shown gross misconduct."

"We're real concerned about safety at the festival tonight," Chief Bartell said.

"That's why the school board acted this morning. We need to put a stop to it," Deevers said.

"We sure don't want tourists getting caught in the crossfire."

Crossfire, Mr. Rodriguez? Are we carrying guns?

Then the big news, sir. Deevers was the one to say it. "Zero tolerance, Dick. Absolutely zero. We won't have gang violence associated with our school. Just so the kids know we're serious, we formally suspended the band program for next year. We'll review the conduct of band members in June 2015 to determine if we're going to support the program going forward. That will put these kids on notice that their current behavior has implications for their future opportunities. It's a teachable moment."

"Holy shit!" I shouted. I looked over at Grandpa. His mouth hung open. His eyes were wide.

"Unfortunate," Dick Kolighter said on the radio.

"They took my band," I shouted. "No band at all next year?"

"This ain't right," Grandpa said. "Not right."

I slammed my fist down on the table. "How about suspending football or cheerleading? Those are the guys throwing rocks through windows, throwing eggs and crap." I thought about school without band and almost got sick. I stood up. "Oh, shit," I said. "Oh, shit. This can't happen."

Grandpa pinched his piehole. "No…but don't do anything stupid, kid."

"Oh, man, Grandpa."

"Breathe, kid."

I turned. I walked down the hall. I went into Dad's bedroom. I had to do something. I had to call Camille and Gore. I had to call RC III. I don't have anybody's number memorized. It's all on my phone. I yanked open Dad's closet to look for my seized property. Dozens of empty 20-ounce pop bottles tumbled out, man. Cokes and Pepsis and root beers. I mean dozens, sir! I'm apparently not the only pop junky in the family. Dad just hides his problem, probably so he doesn't have to give any to me. "Shit!" I shouted. "Shit!" I stomped and crushed and kicked the crap out of all those bottles.

Then I stopped. Then I took several deep breaths.

Thought about our research project, about the cash I spent, the stealing to feed my habit, the shakes from the damn sugar, how sick I got the night before from drinking Dew—and I thought, *I'm getting our money back. I'm going to give it all back to the burners, dorks, geeks, and fat asses.*

Duh, man. Ms. Feagan is right. This isn't about kids. It's about the damn pop machine! That's why I robbed the bastard! That machine is not some emotionally crippled little girl. It's the root of all the trouble! My fat ass, my band getting its ass handed to it! I decided to fight that damn machine! I decided to redistribute all the money back to the people, back to the kids, just like freaking Robin Hood, man!

I stole from Kaus Company and the cheerleaders. Sure. I admit it.

I ran downstairs and opened Mom's computer. I googled breaking into pop machines. I sat in silent deliberation, made big plans, rested, meditated, waited for night. And then under the cover of darkness, I went into the school and did the deed. Rode my bike through the dark. Robbed all eighteen bucks out of that stupid machine. Went down to Cub Foods to buy myself some fruit (because it wasn't enough money to give back to anybody). Got arrested and police brutalized by Officer Rex McCoy, that dick.

And that's why we're here, sir. That's the whole story.

What are you doing?

Why in the hell are you laughing at me?

I do have a bike. Dad doesn't know crap!

Somebody must've left the school open. I just walked in.

They worked. The instructions you pulled out of my hoodie worked. I opened that pop machine!

I don't care if the instructions are for opening a 1970s pop machine. They totally worked!

Oh, no? You don't believe me?

Yeah! Yeah! Let's take a break! Go fill your belly with a cold drink! Hopefully, I'll burst into flames and be a pile of dust when you get back. That'd be better than sitting in this freaking room with a laughing donkey jackass!

CHAPTER 27

So? You know who Baba Obi is, huh?

That's what we called her fat dog, Babs. It's a fake Star Wars name.

How long have they been here, Mr. Rodriguez?

I don't understand why Gore is here at all. She didn't do anything! Oh, crap. This is what she gets for hanging with me. She probably hates me now.

Did you know they were here? Did you know what they were saying? Is that why you kept taking calls and taking breaks?

Are they together?

So there are four rooms with four lawyers all recording our comments and each of the four of us have been making total asses of ourselves trying to protect each other, huh?

What a crappy endeavor, sir. No offense.

Well, actually, total offense, okay?

More laughing?

Mr. Kaus gets here in twenty minutes? And then what? Lock up all us criminals?

No. Almost everything is true that I've told you. Ninety-six percent. Right up through the point in time when I kicked those stupid pop bottles in my Dad's closet. That's all true.

Sure, fine, I left out almost all mention of Kailey.

You'd have to ask RC III about that stuff. I wasn't there for their long walks through the woods out at Fort Neillsen. He knows all about Kailey's trouble.

RC III did talk about her to me, yes. Several times last week. Kailey, Kailey, Kailey. He did tell me she wasn't like those other girls. I knew that but didn't know that. Kailey Kaus laughed when I ass-danced, Mr. Rodriguez. She was part of the culture that robbed me of my dignity.

Yeah, I knew right away who Baba Obi was, but I didn't care. It didn't matter to me that Kailey Kaus was sorry.

Really. At first, I didn't even know what she was sorry about. Kailey found out before I did that her mom, as president of the school board, had steered all the pop money out of the band budget. Once I knew what was up, Kailey could go suck it, you know? Baba Obi can suck it.

I found my phone in a shoe box on a shelf over Dad's hanging clothes. I also found a bunch of bags of potato chips and Doritos and all sorts of candy bars. Dad hoards food, man. What a disaster that guy is.

The phone was dead. I took it downstairs and plugged it in. It was 1:30, I guess. About that time. There were a couple messages from Camille. She was freaking out about the tomato plants out on their farm. The ones Seth and those guys smashed. She screamed, blamed me for not following the plan, for not just doing a fund-raising concert. Later, she called to thank me for the poem I sent her.

Why the hell are you laughing? Good God, sir. This is not funny stuff.

Don't "bah" at me! You already know Camille isn't Baba Obi.

Just keep it to yourself.

The third message was from Gore. She'd left it just a few minutes earlier. Like one o'clock or something. She talked really fast. She said, "Dear Gabe. It's been a Kaus-filled hour at the donut shop. Mrs. Kaus came in looking for 'the fat pornographer.' (I think she was referring to you. She ripped into me too by the way and called my dad a miscreant and I almost slapped her. But Dante threw her out just in time.) Then Kailey showed up. She was looking for you too. You are very popular with Kaus women. Hey, are you in trouble? Is your dad angry? Why aren't you picking up? I want you to call me Gore by the way. I like that name. Sorry I got mad yesterday. I love you too. Please call Dante's if you get this before 2. Call RC III if you don't get this until later. Kailey would like to talk to you. She's still out front. She won't leave the shop. I'm very uncomfortable. Oh, sorry about the band. I can't believe it. Bye."

I didn't know what to think. Kailey? Did she want to beat the crap out of me for that Kaus-gasm video? That would be weird because she really isn't like Janessa and Emily. She's actually really quiet. She doesn't talk in class. She doesn't say crap to people in the halls. She isn't the kind of person who would pick a fight, even if she's insulted. Her parents do all the fighting for her. They're rabid. I mean, her mom is. I guess Mr. Kaus is divorcing Kailey's mom. It's all a big mess.

Anyway, I took a deep breath and made the call. This is totally crazy. (Kailey clearly went crazy.) Kailey answered Dante's Donuts phone. "Where are you?" she asked.

"Who is this?"

"Where are you, Gabe? Are you at home?"

"Uh, yeah?"

"This is Kailey."

"Oh…okay?"

"Don't leave. Stay hidden. Chandra will come get you. We'll see you at Fort Neillsen. Six o'clock."

"Who? Who will see me? I don't think so."

"Shh," Kailey said. "It's okay. Bye, Gabe."

There were a few things about this phone call I didn't like. One, was Kailey going to bring the whole Minnekota jock establishment down on my head? Was she setting up an ambush and had somehow coerced Gore into doing her bidding? Two, Dad would be home by five. How in the hell could I get out of the house for my potentially epic beating? Dad would be watching, right? Three, why did we have to go all the way out to Fort Neillsen? That place is crawling with tourists. Nobody from Minnekota actually goes there.

Yeah, that was the point. Nobody from town goes there.

A minute later, I called Dante's again. This time, Dante answered. "Hey, no more drama. Stop calling here, Chunk."

"Dante!" I shouted. "I'm sorry about my dad! I didn't mean to miss work! Don't fire me, okay?"

"You're not fired. Just stop calling! I had to kick Kailey Kaus out of here. I had to kick her mom out an hour ago. I'm tired of it. Enough drama! I'm a business, not a soap opera!" Dante hung up.

I texted RC III, What's going on?

It took him twenty minutes to get back to me. It's cool. See you at the park. We have to run some errands after work.

Again with the *we*. I texted him back, Who is we?

RC III didn't respond. Man, I wish Gore had a cell phone. What a pain in the ass. I was forced to sit around for several hours, waiting and waiting for what? The only news that came through Facebook was that Mike Timlin and Raj Weigel were arrested for having a ton of illegal fireworks in the back of Mike's car. I know the cops think they were using those fireworks for Geekers stuff, but it's just as likely they were going someplace to blow up mailboxes for no apparent reason. Those dudes are always carrying around nutty crap.

Around 4:30, Dad came home from the college. He didn't speak to me. Grandpa cooked a super heavy meal: spaghetti with bacon Alfredo sauce.

I think he cooked it because he thought it would knock Dad out. Dad wolfs stuff like that down. We sat to eat. Dead silence. Grandpa stared at me and then stared at Dad. We both ate.

"Are you two going to speak? You have some things to say, I imagine," Grandpa said.

Dad set down his fork, looked at me, and said, "Sure. I have something to say. I spoke to your mother this morning, Gabe."

"What now?" Grandpa asked.

"You did what?" I asked.

"She's very disappointed in you, very concerned."

"Oh, really?" I said. "How concerned?"

"Extremely concerned."

"She's going to come home? She's going to spank me maybe?"

"No. But get ready. She's going to call this evening."

"Great. I look forward to that."

"She's calling here?" Grandpa said. "How's that?"

After what Grandpa told me earlier in the day, I actually didn't believe Dad. I thought, *You lie—*

I stared down at my uneaten Alfredo. "Screw this. I'm done. I'm going to bed."

Grandpa eyeballed me.

Dad said, "Be ready for that call."

I went downstairs. I paced and worried. Mom? Could it be real? Did she have a change of heart? Was she really worried about me? What the hell would I even say to her? Where would I speak to her? In my sad basement? When would she call? Would she call the home phone or my cell? It would have to be the home phone because Dad thought he had my cell! *Oh, crap.* And worse, Gore would be at the house to get me sometime in the next thirty minutes. *Maybe you shouldn't go with Gore. Maybe you need to stay home. Maybe—*Then I thought, *Holy balls! Get out of the fudge river, Gabe! Screw this!*

No, no, she didn't call, sir. I asked Grandpa this morning when they came in. It was a lie, I'm sure. Jesus. Justin's mom is right. My dad is emotionally controlling or abusive or whatever. If he convinced me that Mom said she was going to call and then she didn't call, wouldn't I learn that Dad is the only person I can trust? Jesus! What did I do to deserve this?

No, I'm okay.

I am. I'm seriously okay, okay? I'm out of the river.

From the basement, I listened. After ten minutes or so, the TV turned on upstairs. That meant Dad had gulped down his slop. There was some chance he'd pass out on the couch before it was go time.

About five minutes later, I climbed the stairs as quietly as I could. I crawled to the end of the hall and looked into the living room. Dad was sitting upright, staring. He wasn't sleeping like he normally would after dinner (especially that dinner). Grandpa sat in the recliner. He saw me. He shook his head "No" like he knew what I was looking for.

I slid back down the steps into my dungeon.

I sat on my bed and stared up at the little slot window on the bathroom side of my room, on the back wall that faces Kailey's old house. I thought about Kailey knocking on that window as a ten-year-old, how I'd slide out to be with her. I hadn't climbed out that little hole since the summer after seventh grade. I was a much, much tinier human being at that point. I looked at my phone. Quarter to six. *Aw, what the hell.*

And so I did it. I pulled off my band hoodie, peeled off my giant red T-shirt. I pulled off my shoes, peeled off my stretchy pants. I opened the window, pushed my clothes out, threw my phone out, and then put the step stool from the bathroom (the one Doris fell off of) under the window and thought, *Do or die, man.*

My head went through easy. My shoulders went through and I was able to grab the edge of this little cracked concrete walk that runs behind our house to the patio. I sucked in my gut as much as I could, pulled as hard as I could, but my gut is big, man. It lodged in. Lodged bad. I figured there was no way. I pulled so, so hard—strained with everything—but I didn't budge. It hurt. Cut. Made it hard to breathe. Didn't seem like I could go backward either. Was Dad going to find me jammed in the window in my underpants? I pulled again, making this *gah!* sound. Didn't work. Didn't seem like there was any way!

Then I noticed the little girl jumping rope on Kailey's old patio. They're new to Minnekota. I think they're the Jensens? The kid's name is Mandy. I hear her mom barking that at her all the time. Anyway, that Mandy girl jumped rope and watched me wiggle in the window. She stopped and stared. Then she dropped the rope and sort of skipped over, little blond head bobbing in the evening light.

"You're stuck," she said when she got to me.

"Yeah," I said, breathing hard. The metal frame was digging in.

"I think you need to go out, not up," she said.

"What?" I huffed.

"You keep going up." (She pointed up with her finger.) "But you need to go out." (She pointed flat.)

"Oh?"

"Uh-huh," she said.

Maybe she's some kind of spatial genius or maybe she played a lot with one of those plastic cube things that kids use to stuff a specific shape in the right-shaped hole. You know what I mean?

Yeah, I had one of those.

Anyway, instead of pulling myself up off the sidewalk, I pulled myself hard across it and sucked in as much as I could, and holy nuts, sir, I started sliding across that sidewalk, totally scraping my gut as I went. But I was moving. It took me about three pulls to yank my way out.

The girl, Mandy, stepped back. I pushed my way up to hands and knees and breathed like I was dying.

She whispered, "You're in your undies." Then she took off running for her house, so I had to move fast. I'm sure she told her parents.

I yanked on my shirt and then took off running, carrying my hoodie, pants, and shoes. I jetted in my boxers through backyards a couple houses down the block and then ran through the McDermott's side yard and went out to the street.

Gore was there. She'd parked several houses down on the other side of our house. I jumped up and down, signaled her. She saw. She put it in reverse and slowly backed up to me. I opened the door. She said, "Oh, my God. Are you okay? Why aren't you wearing pants?"

"Ow," I grumbled and Gore took off.

"Are you bleeding?"

My forearms were bleeding, but I was overtaken by pride. "I fit through the window in my basement!" I shouted.

"Sort of fit," Gore said. "Looks like you sort of got stuck too." She turned on Park Street and headed toward the lake.

"What are we doing?" I asked.

"I don't know. But I trust RC III," Gore said.

"Uh-huh," I said. Then off we rolled to Fort Neillsen. I pulled on my pants. I pulled on my band hoodie.

Yeah. I'd maybe said it a couple times to him. I did. I told RC III I'd like to break into that stupid machine and take our money back. It was my idea. At least in concept, okay? Those machines are sealed like bank vaults. The school was locked at night. How could I steal anything from that machine?

It was a windy afternoon. Temperature dropped from the 80s on Friday to the 60s. There were some pretty good white caps on the lake as we drove along County B. We got out to Fort Neillsen, which is a resort, not a real park. It's private. Gore parked the car on a gravel lot. I followed her into the snack bar, this cabin with big windows right by the shoreline. It was packed because the wind was keeping Richie Rich Twin Cities resort guests from swimming and boating and junk. I saw RC III in the corner. There was this tiny figure in a pink hoodie sitting across the table from him.

Kailey is small.

I sat down next to RC III. Gore sat down next to Kailey. Gore dwarfed her. Gore could crush her like a mosquito. Kailey pulled back her hood and nodded at me.

"Yeah," I said. "Hi, there."

"I'm the worst best friend you've ever had," Kailey said.

"We're not friends," I said.

"No," Kailey said. She started tearing up. "We're best friends. We've always been best friends."

"You two?" Gore said, shaking her head. "How?"

Kailey didn't address Gore. She spoke straight to me. "I get pushed around by my mom. I get pushed around by Janessa. I'm so tired of it. I'm so tired of all of these people, Gabe. Oh, my God. I don't want to take your band away." She started swallowing hard, trying to talk through these little cries. "I want to be in your band."

I really don't think she wants to be in the band, but that's pretty sweet of her to say.

She took a deep breath. "Okay. I also don't want that crappy lady getting paid," Kailey said. "Ms. Clark is my mom's college friend and she's worse than my mom, even more stupid and mean."

"Big Boobs?" I asked.

Kailey nodded.

"Kailey would like to get your money back," RC III said. "You've been talking about breaking into that pop machine."

"I was joking."

"This is no joke, dude," RC III said. "We can go into the school and do that. I can get you inside."

"I have a key and codes to the pop machine," Kailey nodded.

"What? I don't think that's a good idea," Gore said. "That's breaking and entering. That's, like, jail time, okay?"

No matter what she's said, hear this right now: Gore didn't do crap, sir. Nothing. She didn't even go up to the school with us. She'd better not be telling anybody that she's some criminal because she's not.

Anyway, Kailey was all about me.

"RC III can let us in. Chandra, you can be in the

car or whatever," Kailey said. "But I just want to do this with Gabe."

"You do?" I asked.

She nodded.

"Oh, no. You two?" Gore said.

"We can use the Force," Kailey said.

I nodded. I whispered, "We were Luke Skywalker and Princess Leia when we were kids."

"Oh," Gore said. She sort of deflated, but Gore has nothing to worry about, you know? Gore is—Gore is the best.

"Baba Obi is dead though," Kailey said.

"I'm very sorry to hear that," I said. "Baba was a good dog."

"You dudes are weird," RC III said.

It was a terrible plan, sir. A suicide mission, you know? There's no way we were just going to waltz into the school at midnight and take that money and leave without anyone knowing about it eventually. Coaches know RC III has a key. And in what way could we return the money to dorks and geeks and fat asses? Would we just put the money in baggies and drop it off in mailboxes? We couldn't give it back to the band either. An anonymous donation of a large sum, maybe half in quarters? No way. And anyway, Shaver was fired and the school had gotten rid of us already. The band couldn't even use the money!

For whatever reason, I didn't care. I was pretty moved by Kailey. She'd decided to blow up her life and stick it to her mom, which is pretty cool (yeah, crazy and dumb…but cool). I mean, she really put herself at risk, you know? She was stealing from her own family, not just from the stupid dance squad.

I guess crazy crap at the Kaus home finally pushed her over the edge this spring. Her mom is more psycho than ever. Her dad has been living in the Cities most of the time. (I didn't know that until yesterday.)

And I *was* in a rage about the band program. I'm so sorry we did this now because I know Ms. Feagan is on the case. Grandpa said she stopped by the house last night to see me. (That's when Dad found out I'd taken off.) But yesterday…Kailey and the band suspension? It was too much. I wanted revenge.

Anyway, we decided Kailey and RC III would pick me up from Gore's at 10:15. I'd go in with Kailey and take the money from the machine. Then they'd drop me and the cash off at Cub Foods just in case we were being followed. (We didn't want the cops to follow RC III back to Gore's and get her in trouble. Apparently, she's here though, right? So she did get in trouble.) Gore would pick me up at 11:15 somewhere around Cub if we weren't already arrested. From there, I'd redistribute the money back to band kids and Geekers.

Great plan. Yeah.

Right before we left, Kailey asked Gore to sit at another table. They leaned in and Kailey spoke. RC III said, "Kailey needs to say a few things to her." When they got up, they hugged. Pretty crazy, sir. They've had a lot of bad blood, Gore threatening to murder Kailey and all. It's better, except for the fact we're locked in a police station.

Before we left, Kailey hugged me around my neck really hard, whispered "I'm sorry. I'm sorry" in my ear. She smells awesome, Mr. Rodriguez.

Sure. Yeah. On the ride home. While she was driving. Gore asked me really quietly while she was staring at the road in front of her. "Do you love Kailey Kaus, Gabe?"

I just turned to her without thinking and said,

"I'm in love. But she's not the one I love, Chandra Wettlinger."

She blushed. I probably did too. Am I blushing right now?

Yeah, my face is hot, man.

Gore also said, "Kailey is different. She's a good person. She isn't what she looks like."

"Neither is RC III," I said.

"Neither are you," Gore said.

"What about you?" I asked.

"No, you're all different, but I'm what I look like," Gore said.

"I've seen you disco dance," I told her.

"Oh…yeah. I'm a little different."

You know what, Mr. Rodriguez? The world is pretty complicated. We can't take anything for granted. My goth girlfriend is a great disco dancer and she's also really good at selling donuts. What other surprises are out there?

Okay. Gore and I hung out at her place.

Dad didn't call me until 10 p.m., after Ms. Feagan left the house. Of course, I didn't answer. RC III and Kailey picked me up right after he called.

No, her dad wasn't around. He was back in the Cities.

I printed the pop machine break-in instructions from the Internet at Gore's place. I hoped to take the fall, you know? I didn't want Kailey or RC III getting in trouble for my war. What do I have to lose? I'd already lost Mom, Dad, Justin, band. Might as well get locked up in juvie. *Maybe juvie has a band program and I can practice my shiny trombone in peace.*

It's true. I do have stuff to lose now. It also occurred to me this morning that the break-in was more Kailey's war than mine.

Right before Kailey and RC III showed, Gore ran upstairs and came back with a *V for Vendetta* mask. You know what I'm talking about?

Yeah. Guy Fawkes! Right!

"This is one of my prized possessions from middle school," Gore said. She handed me the mask. "Wear it well."

"Oh, I don't know," I said, staring down at it. "I don't think so."

"Please, Gabe. Will you at least try not to get caught? I just found you."

"Yeah. I guess," I said. I guess we knew the break-in was a dumb idea.

"Good." She kissed my cheek. She smells great too, sir, like lemonade and fall at the same time. Really different from Kailey's hair products. She whispered, "See you in an hour."

RC III and Kailey pulled into the driveway.

When I climbed in the car, Kailey said, "What's that?"

"Vendetta?" I said.

"No, dude," RC III said. "If somehow we get videotaped, they'll see that mask and think one of your Geeker computer dudes is the thief. No masks. If we get caught, we get caught and we tell the story of why we did it."

"Yeah? Why exactly *are* you doing this?" I asked.

"Pops always tells me not to get too fond of the benefits of this crap system," RC III said. "Guess I'm not too fond of the crap system generally."

I didn't know what to say to that, sir. But I liked it. Gave me courage.

"Okay. Even if I wore a mask, they'd recognize my body," I said. "No masks. We'll go naked as the day we were born."

"Keep your pants on, man," RC III giggled.

We drove through town in silence. Kailey reached

over the seat and we sort of shook hands, held hands for a couple seconds.

RC III dropped Kailey and me off on the street in front of the school. We ran along the dark edge of the parking lot toward the west door—the one RC III's key opens. Before she opened the door, Kailey turned to me. "Sorry I've been a bitch," she said.

"No, no…you're pretty cool," I said.

"Uh-huh. Not really. But now I'm with the leader of the rebellion."

"Yeah?"

"Gabe Skywalker," Kailey said. Then she smiled like she did when we were little kids in her driveway. She looked like that little girl, sir. She looked like my Leia with her blond cinnamon bun hair.

No, she didn't have cinnamon bun hair. I could just see it. Picture what it was. The moon lit up her amazing face. She reached up and touched my cheek. She nodded. She swallowed really hard. She said, "I'm really sorry I went to the dark side."

"I did too, just in a different way," I said. "Are you ready for this?"

She blinked. Turned. Pulled RC III's key out of her pocket, stuck it in the lock, and we were in.

We cruised up over the gym through the weight room. Then down the side stairs and out the door that opens into the cafeteria. The only light came from the machine, sir. It cast a bright halo around itself. We slowed and shuffled around the edge of the tables in the dark. We got to the machine. Kailey popped this bike lock–style key into it, turned it, and the front panel came open. Then she plugged a code into a little keyboard. We were Luke and Leia opening a security door in the Death Star. The machine released with this suctioned sigh and the interior door opened.

"Shit," I said. "We did it."

"Yeah, we did," Kailey whispered.

Of course, we're stupid as hell. We didn't have a bag to put the money in. Luckily, the change box only contained sixteen quarters.

Yeah, great luck, huh?

There were fourteen dollar bills in the dollar box.

"Oh, my God. Was this machine already robbed?" Kailey said. "This is my machine to rob! There's nothing here."

"It's okay," I said. "Just being in here means a lot. This is cool."

"Screw this machine," Kailey said. She kicked it.

"Yeah," I said. I took two steps back and then kicked it hard.

Didn't do crap. The thing is built like an armored truck.

"Let's go," Kailey said. She left the pop machine's door open and walked fast back toward the stairs to the weight room.

"Don't you want to lock it back up?" I called after her.

"No," she shouted.

So I followed. I could barely keep up. Girl is light on her feet. Kailey was also significantly pissed, Mr. R., which is why I realized she's fighting her own war.

When we got out to the car, she gulped for air. Her eyes looked like bullets in the moonlight. I climbed in back. Kailey climbed into the front seat. She looked at RC III and talked fast. "They aren't supposed to empty machines this time of the month. Somebody already took the money."

"I'm sure your dad had it emptied."

"No!" Kailey shouted. "Couldn't happen."

"There wasn't anything?" RC III asked.

"Eighteen bucks," I said. "It's the gesture that counts though. That you guys would do this is huge. It's awesome. We're all good."

"No, we're not good," Kailey whispered. "I'm not good." She sighed really hard.

I actually felt relieved that we didn't get a felony haul, you know?

RC III drove across town. As we neared the Cub parking lot, Kailey turned around in her seat and said, "Can I call you tomorrow? Can we talk? Do you want to hang out?"

"I'm grounded. Bad," I said. "Maybe forever."

"After that, we can hang out?" Kailey said. "Me, you, RC III, and Chandra?"

"Yeah. Yeah," I nodded. "Definitely."

"Hey, you guys, we're there. Gabe, get ready to get out," RC III said.

RC III pulled into the back of the parking lot, slowed down. Kailey said, "I'm serious. You're Gabe Skywalker."

I nodded. I smiled. I gave the thumbs-up. I climbed out.

I watched RC III and Kailey pull away.

The quarters jingled in my stretchy pants pocket. The fourteen dollars were crumpled in my hand. Gore wouldn't be around to get me for twenty minutes. I walked down one of the parking lot rows toward the front door of Cub. Thought I'd get a vitamin water, maybe a banana. *Maybe buy a good-bye gift for Mr. Shaver? Cigarettes? Ha-ha!* I thought about Kailey wanting to hang out. I thought about how two weeks earlier, I was an ass-dancing fool. I thought about how strong my legs felt after working out for a week. I thought about how maybe I really was Gabe Skywalker, leader of the rebellion!

And then the small-town Minnekota bullshit.

A car rolled up from behind, slow. I looked over my right shoulder. Seth Sellers had his window down. He had a black eye from the Geeker beating. "Hey there, fudge balls," he said. "Nice to see you, man."

"Oh, shit," I whispered. My heart accelerated.

I leaned forward. Justin was in the passenger seat. He stared straight forward. Janessa and Emily Yu were in the backseat. Janessa glared at me, her middle finger extended.

"Back at you, Janessa," I said.

"We'd like to talk to you about the fake beaver shots you're making," Seth said.

"Yeah, you fat-ass dick," Janessa hissed.

"I already apologized to Janessa and I didn't make those pics," I said. "Anyway, I'm here for groceries, not talk."

I sped up. I just had to make it into the store. Seth wouldn't chase me in there. The car moved as fast as me, of course, so I took off. I ran. Without Grandpa's workouts, I couldn't run like that. I cut between cars and heard Seth's car roar and his tires squeal. I just had to cross the strip right in front of the store and I'd be in. I heard Seth's car skid to a halt.

Somebody yelled, "Gabe Johnson. Stop where you are. Stop running."

I looked to my left. Officer Rex McCoy slid off the back of his cop car. He was holding a donut. I shit you not. I turned to my right and ran like hell. RC III and Kailey were close by. I needed to give them time to get away! As I ran, I looked over my shoulder. Officer McCoy, who is fatter than me, was giving chase. *You can do this!* I thought. I turned on my afterburners, which don't really work that well. Then

I heard faster footsteps. I looked again. Seth Sellers was chasing me. He was closing fast. And Justin was right behind him. *Oh, shit!* I shot past the liquor store and down the strip mall strip. I got in front of the dry cleaner, almost to Subway, before Seth caught me. He jumped on my back and knocked me forward. One of the sixteen quarters shot out of my pocket and rolled in front of me right as my face bounced on the pavement. I screamed. Seth grabbed my arm and wrenched it around my back. "You fat pussy!" he shouted. "You want to mess with me?"

I didn't think twice, just rolled with all my might. Seth crashed over to my left. I balled up my fistful of fourteen bucks, pulled it back into mammoth punching position, said, "You're a waste of space!"

Just then, Justin jumped on top of Seth and pinned him down hard. "Run, Gabe!" he yelled.

"What are you doing?" Seth screamed.

Justin's pretty strong, I guess. I pushed myself up onto my feet but paused so I could watch Seth wriggle under Justin Cornell's superior strength because it was awesome to see. Justin smiled at me and I wanted to high-five him because damn, I really do love him!

"Go!" Justin shouted.

Just then, Officer McCoy crashed into me.

That's how I scraped my legs. McCoy's knees crushed into my calves. I've never felt pain like that, sir. I screamed so loud.

McCoy sounded like he was going to die he was breathing so hard. "What in the hell is going on here?" He pushed his weight on top of me, smashing me. My chest, belly, and elbow scrapes from climbing out the basement window slid on the concrete.

"Ah!" I cried. Then I thought of RC III and Kailey. "I stole the money! I stole the money! Here!" I stretched my arm up. I uncurled my fingers. The fourteen dollars from the machine fell out of my hand.

"You stole what?" McCoy shouted.

"The money!" I shouted.

McCoy stayed on top of me. He spoke into his little radio on his shoulder. "Send a couple cars down to Cub. We got ourselves a little Spunk River ruckus going on. Gabe Johnson. Seth Sellers. Apprehended both."

With that, Seth ripped himself away from Justin and took off running.

"Assailant in flight!" McCoy cried. "Seth Sellers fleeing!"

They got him? Good. Ass wipe.

Janessa got a disorderly conduct? Whoa. She's mean, dude. I wouldn't want to try cuffing her.

Yeah, McCoy was looking for me. Not because of the pop machine. Dad realized I'd escaped when Ms. Feagan showed up. Dad didn't even try to find me himself. Grandpa told me this morning he couldn't stop Dad. Dad called the cops. They were all looking for me because of Dad. In the car, Officer McCoy said, "Nobody cares about your fourteen-dollar theft." He's an idiot, man. A theft is a theft. Cops cared about the theft this morning, didn't they? They were crazy about it. They tried to get me to admit to robbing a bunch of machines!

What? Are you kidding? What the hell?

Thirteen thousand dollars? From pop machines? Last night? How?

Yeah. J. D. Carlson is Kailey's cousin. He's a huge meth-head dirtbag though. Not a good guy.

She…she was really pissed that there wasn't money in the machine we robbed. I don't think she'd help J. D. Do you guys think Kailey took all that money?

No, I didn't notice us being surveilled at Fort Neillsen. Is that why Gore and RC III were picked up this morning? Kailey was being watched?

Oh, Kailey. Oh, crap. Is she going to be put away? Like big time?

Of course. Kailey works for the business. She runs the Kaus pop stands at Jaycees events and crap. Does that mean it's not a crime for her to empty the machines?

Up to her dad, huh? I don't really know him. When will he be here again?

What's that paper?

It's for me? From Kailey? Let me see it!

Ha. Wow. She says, "Use the Force, Gabe."

Can you get something back to her?

The Force runs strong in our family.

Yes, sir. Thanks, Mr. Rodriguez.

Yeah, I'm in total shock. I had no idea. I'm—

Yes. Seriously. Why have you been laughing all day, Mr. R.? Tell me something funny. I need it bad. Tell me your funny story.

They were making out? On stage at school? This morning? Justin and Camille? A flock of sheep? What?

Two sheep. That's plenty. That's about what would fit in Justin's car.

Arrested? Are they okay?

I'm so glad. I'll clean the sheep poop myself if Deevers just forgets about this part. Wow.

Yeah! Yeah! That's hilarious! I figured right away they had to be Camille's sheep. I just couldn't for a second figure out how they got in the school. Of course, Justin has a key. Student council officers get keys. Why did they do it?

Whoa. That's one badass protest. *Geekers won't be sheep*. Pretty sweet. I shouldn't have been hard on them. I love those guys.

Balls. This has been the craziest few days ever, right? Nothing's ever going to be the same again.

It's all so crazy, man.

Mr. Rodriguez?

Am I ever going to be able to go home?

No, I don't want to see Dad. I just want to go to bed. In my bed.

Seriously. Seriously. Please. I want to go home, sir.

When will Mr. Kaus be here?

CHAPTER 28

THREE DAYS LATER, WEDNESDAY, JUNE 19, 2:30 P.M.

FINAL INTERVIEW CONDUCTED AT BITTERROOT COFFEE SHOP, MINNEKOTA, MN.

I don't mind if you record this, Mr. Rodriguez. You've been really cool. Really good to us. All you guys. Thanks.

Yeah, I'm grounded! Grandpa is trying to stay hidden, but he's over there at that table by the window, keeping an eye on me. Yeah, hi, Grandpa. He's pretending to read.

I get it. I stayed out all night one night and then broke out of being grounded the next night and got arrested for robbing a pop machine. That's some highly groundable business.

Dad's okay. He's letting me go to work. I really have to go because RC III's dad sent him to Georgia to work construction with his uncle for the rest of the summer. He'll be back in the fall. His dad actually likes it here apparently. I already miss him.

Dante needs workers. You know anybody?

Well, I'm experiencing my fifteen minutes of fame. I think Dad's sort of proud of me.

Did you see that headline? Front page of the Fargo paper, right? "Fat Boy vs. the Cheerleaders." *The Star Tribune* from Minneapolis is a little more politically correct. "Minnekota Student Confronts Corrupt School Board."

I like the fat boy headline better. It's funnier. The article got picked up by all kinds of news services because of that headline. The reporter from the Fargo paper let me talk about our pop research from health class too. I got to mention poor kids who don't have breakfast and suck down the poison to stay awake. So "fat boy" works, sir. Better laugh than cry in this case because fat boy is a sexy headline. And sexy sells, gets the story out there.

That's what Gore tells me anyway.

She's right. Dad's been taking calls from TV stations all day today. They all want to talk to the fat boy. Ha-ha.

I shit you not, Mr. R.

No, none of this would've happened, except for Randall Andersson. Because Ms. Feagan was his favorite teacher, Randall and Ms. Feagan went out for dinner on Saturday night (while I was escaping through the tiny window). Feagan had already spent Saturday winding up all the old ladies in town about the band. At dinner, Randall said he planned to bring me on stage during Sunday's Wall of Sound Spunk River concert. He said he'd make a huge stink about the band trouble in front of everybody. He told Feagan he wanted me to give a speech.

That's why Ms. Feagan showed up at my house on Saturday night. She came by to prep me. Of course, by that time I was just about to climb in RC III's car so that me and Kailey could do the dirty deed. Dad looked for me all over the house. Then he called the cops. He was out of his mind apparently.

While I was spending my day with you at the police station, Randall and Ms. Feagan visited Dad at the house to tell him that even though robbing the machine was stupid, I was right to rebel generally. Randall convinced Dad to bring me to the concert if I got out of jail in time.

That was one of the calls you took? From Dad?
Okay.

After Kailey's parents set us all free (did you see
Mrs. Kaus? She looked like she'd been run over by a
truck), Dad and Grandpa drove me straight to Spunk
River Days. I was not expecting that and I wasn't very
happy about it. I hadn't slept and my body scrapes were
all burning up and my stretchy pants were sliding down
my butt because I didn't eat almost anything for like
30 hours and I'd already been dropping weight before
that. I was all like, "No! I don't want to go! Take me
home! Lock me in the basement, please!"

Dad didn't respond. Grandpa said, "You gotta see
this through, buddy."

And so I did.

There were five thousand people at Wilson Beach.
That's bigger than the whole town of Minnekota, man.
Wall of Sound is a big deal. Security guys at the event
just kept nodding and waving us through the sea of
people. Dad drove me right up behind the band shell.

I got out of the car and there they all were—Austin
in his sagging shorts (like my stretchies), Tess in her
bikini top, Schae and Omar and Caitlyn and everybody.

Yeah. Everybody. Justin and Camille too. Those guys had their instruments in one hand and were holding hands with the other. I sort of cried when I saw them. We all hugged pretty hard. Justin has to pay off all these repairs to his dad's car interior. Sheep hooves cut right through the fabric, I guess.

Everybody cheered when I got there too, which is also maybe what made me cry.

It's all sort of a blur. Ms. Feagan was back there. She pulled me aside and said I was on tap to give a short speech. I shrugged. The concert started. There were so many people, I could barely move. But everyone danced, which I liked. Wall of Sound played for forty-five minutes or so. Then Randall Andersson stopped singing and started talking about how important music programs were to him growing up. How he always had a hard time talking, always felt awkward, out of place, like a total outsider in his own hometown until Barry Shaver stuck a trombone in his hand. When he said the name Barry Shaver, everyone in the crowd cheered like crazy. Mr. Shaver has a lot of support in Minnekota, even if he acted like an idiot. Then Randall said, "In the past few weeks, there's been a concerted effort to remove music from the high school here in the Lake Area." People booed for about a minute straight. The booing was so loud, I could feel it vibrating in my chest. "But your kids wouldn't take it. They wouldn't accept their fate. Your kids stood up!" The boos turned to cheers. All the Geekers slapped me on the back. "Allow me to introduce you to Gabriel Johnson, leader of the resistance, and the rest of the Minnekota Lake Area High School Band!" All five thousand people screamed.

I stood back there behind the band shell, totally stunned, sir. I couldn't process, you know? Then Justin put his hand on my shoulder and shouted in my ear, "Get moving, man! Go!"

I climbed up the steps. The Geekers climbed up behind me. The audience cheered like crazy. Randall handed me a mic. The sun set over the lake, so everything turned orange. I scanned the crowd in front of me. Ms. Feagan stood next to Dad right up front. And Gore and her dad stood next to Grandpa. Gore was just spilling tears too. I gave her a big smile and swallowed and looked out across the whole town of faces and just said, "We love you guys! The MLAHS band loves you. Everybody. It's been such a crazy few days. We didn't mean to do any harm at all. We don't want to stop anyone from doing what they love, okay? We want the cheerleaders to dance and…and we want RC III out there throwing touchdowns for the football team. We don't want to take anything away from anyone because we all need our thing. Geekers have to geek out, right?"

The crowd whooped.

But seriously. "We really need our thing. So much. We're a band. We play music. We need to keep being a band! Thank you!"

I know. Not the greatest speech. But I didn't want to go on and on, you know?

"How about a little rendition of 'Tequila,' Gabe?" Randall Andersson asked.

"Yeah. Yeah," I nodded. "Let's do it!"

Then Austin and Omar started pounding their drums and Jake from Wall of Sound started pounding along. Then Randall began directing. He gestured like Mr. Shaver and everybody on stage laughed. Then everybody in my band and his band (except me because I didn't have my 'bone) raised their instruments and then *bam*. My band and Wall of Sound played the greatest version of "Tequila" ever played.

Everybody danced. Everybody whooped and spun around. Everybody shouted "Tequila" at the right moment. All five thousand, including Gore, my dad, and my grandpa.

Pretty amazing.

Wall of Sound played another few songs. We slid back down the back steps. I had reporters from a few papers grab me right away. They'd already talked to Ms. Feagan. They'd talked to Chief Bartell. They knew all about the Spunk River War. They knew that I'd sent apology notes to the cheerleaders about the dirty pics. I told the story about the pop machine, how it nearly killed me. I told them about robbing it but how it wasn't a robbery because Kailey Kaus was protesting with us and I said that she and J. D. Carlson were returning all the money. (I made that part up. Turns out J. D. couldn't return all the money because he'd already spent some of it by the time he was arrested Sunday.) I said that I was tired of being called names and that I'd learned how crappy it is to call people names in general. Even if you think those people don't care, they care and it hurts and robs people of their dignity. I sure hated being called a lard ass. I'm sure the cheerleaders didn't enjoy getting called cheer bitches. I think that's where the "Fat Boy vs. the Cheerleaders" headline came from. I told that story. But didn't the Fargo reporter understand me? I don't like getting called names!

Ha-ha. Right. Better laugh than cry. In this case.

Yeah, I talked to RC III Monday. He said, "Pops heard you on the radio. Says you should be proud."

I guess RC III's pops doesn't think RC III should be proud. He flew to Atlanta on Tuesday.

I haven't heard at all from Kailey. Do you know what's happening with her?

Justin told me last night that the dance school has a "For Sale" sign in front of it.

What about Gore?

Am I blushing?

Since I'm grounded, she's coming over for dinner tonight. She came over last night too. And Monday night. Me, her, and Grandpa hung out in the backyard. We had some lemonade. Grandpa was a little freaked out by her black clothes and fingernails and stuff. He definitely likes her though. "You don't raise your voice and squawk like a chicken much, do you?" he asked her last night.

"No," she said.

"I appreciate that."

Speaking of Grandpa. He's flapping the banana hammock at us. See that?

Waving it. We ran two miles yesterday. We're swimming today, doing the Spunk River Challenge.

Oh, man. Oh, man. Why didn't I get a new suit? I'm going to strangle my boys again? I'm going to go all beached whale on it again?

Yeah. Ha-ha. It's worth it. Of course, Mr. Rodriguez. Who cares?

I'm in control of my dignity. I have my dignity, for sure.

Thanks, sir. Thanks again for your help.

Time to swim. Take care, Mr. R.

AFTERWORD

The preceding document was submitted to Minnesota's Seventh District Court as part of a successful lawsuit against the Minnekota Lake Area School Board, which led to the reinstatement of the high school's band program and a pending review of the release of its director, Barry Shaver.

Regarding the vending machine break-in, no charges were ever filed against Robert Carter, Chandra Wettlinger, Kailey Kaus, or Gabriel Johnson. Rick Kaus, the CEO of the Kaus Company, submitted that Kailey was simply doing her job by collecting the money. Because Robert Carter had a key to the school and no district policy exists against athletes using the school after hours, no charges of trespassing were leveled.

Regarding other items related to the so-called Spunk River War, Seth Sellers and Janessa Rogers received fines for disorderly conduct. Mike Timlin and Raj

Weigel pled guilty to a variety of misdemeanor charges, including petty theft and possession of illegal fireworks. Sentencing is pending. Camille Gardener and Justin Cornell received fines for trespassing and vandalism. They drove two sheep to the MLA High School in the backseat of Justin's car. Justin is paying for repairs to said car in a private settlement with his parents.

Katherine Kaus, who chaired the school board during its ruling on vending proceeds, its decision to fire band director Barry Shaver, and its ruling that suspended the MLAHS band program, resigned from her post in the week following the upheaval. Although the Kaus Company continues operations in Minnekota, Katherine Kaus, her husband, Rick, and her daughter, Kailey, have since relocated to another state in order to refocus on the marriage and the family.

Brian Deevers wrote a letter of apology to the community and remains the principal of MLA High School.

Because of Gabriel Johnson's activism, the offending pop machine has been removed from the high school cafeteria. A tenth of a percent increase in county property taxes will be on the ballot in the fall. The increase is intended to fund summer marching camp, a dance team, and, most importantly, a healthy breakfast program for all school-aged members of the district. According to a poll published in MLJournal.com, the increase has support from 77 percent of likely voters.

Note:

When Gabriel said during his follow-up interview that he was experiencing fifteen minutes of fame, he was correct. The *Fat Boy vs. the Cheerleaders* story faded quickly. I doubt very much that he's bothered by this fact.

The last time I saw Gabriel, walking the Lakeshore Path during Minnekota's July Water Sports Festival, he looked healthy and content. He wore shorts. He held hands with a very tall girl in all black. He smiled at me, nodded, and then strolled away into the fading light.

I thought, *We did good work.*

—Henry P. Rodriguez, Attorney at Law

ACKNOWLEDGMENTS

Thanks so much to my fantastic agent, Jim McCarthy. He's guided me through so many projects now. One day, we'll be old, Jim. This book couldn't have happened without the guidance of Leah Hultenschmidt (I miss you!) and Todd Stocke. I'm so thankful to all the support and encouragement I receive from so many great people at Sourcebooks. On the home front, Stephanie Wilbur Ash is the best to hang with. I'm so lucky. She fires my imagination and makes me cry laughing. Leo, Mira, Christian, and Charlie, you are smart and hilarious and a source of unending inspiration. Speaking of inspiration, thank you to the kids of the Hillsboro School District, Hillsboro, Wisconsin, for the great messages of support you sent during the writing of this book. (Hillsboro is excellent and hilly.) Finally, thank you to the students and faculty of Minnesota State University, Mankato. I so appreciate your curiosity, energy, and kindness.

Like Gabe Johnson?
Meet Felton Reinstein.
Don't miss the summer he
went from joke to jock in

Geoff Herbach's
STUPID FAST

CHAPTER 1: NOW

This could be a dark tale!

It's not.

I don't think so.

Maybe.

I can't sleep. It's 1:03 a.m. Almost September. The weather is warm, even though it's football season. There's this huge moon in the sky, but I can't see it from the basement, where my bedroom is. I saw it plenty.

Tonight.

Dark tale? My dad did commit suicide.

Not so dark? I'm me. I hop up and down.

Where to start?

Not in the '70s, when Jerri was a little girl. Not ten years ago, when I was five and found Dad dead in the garage. How about last November?

I should really be exhausted. But I'm not.

I, Felton Reinstein, stand on my bed because I can't sleep.

Go.

CHAPTER 2:
MY BODY
GREW HAIR

I am not stupid funny. I am stupid fast.

My last name is Reinstein, which is not a fast name. But last November, while I was a sophomore, my voice finally dropped, and I grew all this hair on my legs (and other places) and then I got stupid fast. I'm serious.

Before my voice dropped in the fall, when my class was outside for gym, I played flag football and felt like trying for some reason. I was pretty good because even though I hadn't yet fully gone through puberty like all the chuckleheads in my grade, and never tried before and wasn't even interested in the slightest, I've always been good at sports (a fact I hid by not trying) but not ridiculously good.

Then Thanksgiving came, and I couldn't stop eating and I couldn't wake up before like noon, which drove Jerri nuts, and I grew taller and got all this crazy hair.

The hair was like corn coming up in June. You look

one day and there are sprouts in the dirt, but mostly, you see dirt, and then like a week later, those sprouts aren't sprouts but corn and are already knee-high and you can't see the dirt at all.

I ate too much at Thanksgiving, about a thousand pounds, and I couldn't wake up in the morning, and I sprouted hair. A week later, I had a thousand pounds of hair everywhere.

Then because my voice dropped, I got moved to baritone for the Christmas concert, which was bad news because I didn't know the parts at all, so I sang the tenor parts except an octave below, which you could totally hear.

And it went on. I kept sleeping and eating, and Jerri yelled at me to get out of bed, and I yelled at Andrew to stop playing the piano so I could sleep. So Jerri yelled at me for yelling at Andrew and I'd get pissed and get out of bed and go to the refrigerator and stuff bread in my mouth because I was so hungry. Then Jerri would yell at me for eating too fast, and Andrew would shout "Felton's a pig!" and on and on all winter—my pants getting too short and my shirts looking shrunken, not covering my belly button, which is gross (Jess Withrow and Abby Sauter told me it was gross), and Jerri and Andrew shouting at me and me shouting back.

Jerri never yelled before November.

And then in the spring, my gym class had to go outside to run the 600 yard dash for some physical fitness test thing (apparently the last one we ever have to do), and I was just mad, all wound up from all the yelling and my clothes not fitting right, and when Coach Knautz, the gym teacher, yelled go, I took off. I ran like an angry donkey, a very fast one, even though I didn't care about winning. I just needed a release. I sprinted all 600 yards. And I beat everybody, even the other fast kids, by about 150 yards. People were screaming, "Look at Rein Stone go!" Peter Yang, my second best friend, whispered, "What happened to you?"

"Hee-haw!" I shouted and pumped my fist.

Peter Yang rolled his eyeballs and walked away.

• • •

Jerri—who happens to be my mom but also a big hippy who doesn't like hierarchy, so she's always had me and Andrew call her by her first name—was all puffy and weird during dinner that night. She was a crossing guard at the middle school at the time. The middle school is right next to the high school but lets out a little earlier so the high school kids don't scare and beat the pee out of the middle school kids. She was out there on the corner when I ran the 600. She saw it. I could hear her screaming from the corner. "Run, Felton! Go! Oh my God!"

"Felton," she said, serving me and Andrew whole grain, organic macaroni and cheese, "Listen. You need to do something about that speed of yours."

"Oh," I said, digging in.

"Are you listening to me? Really, Felton. That speed is a gift…from the Universe…and I know you need to be who…need to be who…" She sat down at the table and stared up at the ceiling.

"Who, Jerri?" I asked.

"I heard you're fast, Felton," Andrew nodded at me.

"I'm eating macaroni here," I said. "Mind your own business."

"You're super fast, Felton Reinstein," Jerri nodded. She spoke really quietly. "It's like you're Jamaican instead of…the son of a small, sad Jewish dude."

She was referring to me and Andrew's father, who was already long dead but was in life—so we were to believe—not built for speed.

I thought for a moment before sticking more macaroni in my face.

"Were you fast, Jerri?"

"No. Not fast. I played guitar and read poetry. You've got a gift from the...from your...from the Universe, Felton."

"I'm not fast either," said Andrew. "Of course, I wouldn't want to be. Athletic prowess is a curse, I think."

"What the hell do you know?" I glared at him. He stared back at me through his big, plastic nerd glasses. "You're a punk middle schooler."

"It's just the way I feel," he said.

"No, Andrew. Wrong," Jerri said.

"I simply think sports are bad for a young man," Andrew said.

"No, goddamn it," Jerri said all hot and red-faced, "We...We have to support...what the Universe provides. Do you understand me?"

"You shouldn't swear, Jerri," Andrew said.

"Just shut up, Andrew," Jerri said.

"Don't say shut up," Andrew shouted back.

"I'm sorry," Jerri said, looking down.

"Dad wasn't a Jamaican Jew, was he?" I asked.

"No," Jerri frowned. "Your father was a sweet, fat American Jew." Then she stood up from the table, walked to the sink, and dropped her bowl of whole grain, organic macaroni into it. I didn't even see her take a bite.

Jerri was acting a little freaky. This might have been a sign to me, but I didn't really pay attention because she was standard issue weird forever (big hippy sandals, organic turnip soup, drumming circles, making us call her Jerri). But freaky? Not really. Well, maybe a little. Sometimes. Off and on.

• • •

Jerri wasn't the only one acting weird. Coach Knautz pulled me out of biology the next day. He knocked on Mr. Willard's door, pointed at me while the whole class stared, and then said he had to have a word in private. Private? That's a gross word. It reminds me of bathrooms and people's privates all hanging out. Gross.

I was scared. I hadn't gotten in trouble since eighth grade, when I took a bathroom stall apart with a screwdriver (totally grounded from TV and suspended for three days, which ended my life of crime and vandalism), and I couldn't imagine why a coach would pull me out of class. He walked me down the hall without saying a word. He took me into the gym offices in total silence. He sat me down across the desk from him and then stared at me and shook his head and breathed through his big nose.

"Yes…uh…sir?" I asked.

"Listen, Reinstein, I have never seen anything like it." (Nose breath.)

"Like what?" I said meekly. I was completely shaking in my shoes because I thought I must've done something horribly terrible.

"I have never seen a kid run so damn fast in the fitness test," he said.

"Ohhhhh," I breathed easier. "Yeah. Jerri is pretty excited."

"Who?"

"My mom."

"Right. Jerri. And she's right to be excited, Reinstein. I've been doing this for twelve years, and I have never seen anything like it. Ken Johnson wasn't even close to as fast as you, and he took two firsts at State last year."

"I know," I said, without any enthusiasm, I might add. Why? Ken Johnson has always been a jerk. The summer after eighth grade, Ken Johnson shoved me off my Schwinn Varsity, which he called a stupid bike because he said my brake lever scratched his car, which maybe it did, but only because he parked like a jerk so I couldn't get my bike past him. Ken Johnson.

"I'm guessing you're a sprinter," Coach Knautz nodded, "just by the way you run. I'm guessing you're really built for 100 meters or maybe 200."

"Maybe," I said, still not knowing what he was getting at.

Mr. Knautz's eyes were watery. He nodded more. He was sweaty.

"You have to do something with your God-given speed. You have to go out for track," he said.

"Oh," I said. I squinted and thought, those locker room lights beating down on my head, *Hmm. Am I going to say yes to this silliness? Hmmmm.* I wouldn't have said yes, but I had Jerri's voice echoing in my head from the macaroni dinner *(the Universe…the Universe…the Universe)*, and I thought about Andrew all arrogant and superior, even though he's just a punk kid, and there was this poster hanging on the wall behind Coach Knautz (I was squinting at it) with this dude running in the desert with the word ACHIEVE underneath him, and I was emotionally moved by it, which is ridiculous, I know, but whatever. And, yes, I wanted Jerri to be proud of me. Andrew has his thing, his piano, which everyone loves him for. Jerri's so proud of Andrew. Jerri has never seemed proud of me. I mean, man, what young son doesn't want his mom to be proud of him even if he has to call her Jerri? (*The Universe, Felton…the Universe…*)

So I said, "Uh, okay, sounds good," which caused Coach Knautz to punch his fist in the air, shout yes, and then try to high-five me.

• • •

So even though track season was half done by that time, and even though I had no intention before to do anything but eat and sleep and grow hair on my body and practice my completely lame and humorless standup routine (I'll get to this later), and even though I've always thought that track is dumb because you just run like you're a scared buffalo getting chased by hyenas on Animal Planet, I joined the team.

It was right to do so.

I was totally nervous about it. The juniors and seniors have always been jerks.

But seriously, I did pretty well.

In fact, right away, it became obvious, even though my last name is Reinstein and not something Jamaican like Bolt or Lightning or Nitro or Napalm, that I'm sincerely fast. Actually, it turned out that I am so fast that I made varsity in the 100 meters, which pissed off a couple of seniors, *boohoo*, but it wasn't my fault. (Coach Knautz kept me off the relays for political reasons, he said.) It turned out I could already run almost as fast as that jerk Ken Johnson.

All the rest of the spring, a growing crowd of sweaty dudes who looked like Coach Knautz—balding, wearing those elastic coach shorts pulled halfway up their fat bellies because they're also coaches, albeit football coaches—kept coming up to me, saying, "I've never seen anything like it. You're what, fifteen?"

All the rest of the spring, Jerri kept yelling from her crossing guard position out on the corner or from the stands at other schools or from next to Andrew at big invitational meets, where I always placed a closer and closer second right behind Ken Johnson. "Run, Felton! Go!" (Even as she got freakier at home.) And all spring long, all the jocks in my grade, especially Cody

Frederick, who I always thought smelled like an old urinal cake in a locker room (sorry), kept saying, "Can't wait for football. You're going out, right, Reinstein? We're going to kick some ass in the fall."

"I guess," I'd tell them.

I did not enjoy the jock bus rides. I missed Gus, my first best friend, who sometimes sat on the hill watching track practice, shaking his head in disapproval. But I loved to run. *Loved it.*

Fast like donkey. Very fast. Zing!

• • •

But then at Regionals, the qualifier for the State meet, because I was filled with donkey adrenaline that made me shake, because I knew—seriously understood—that I'd gotten as fast as that jerk Ken Johnson and I had a good shot at beating him and making him feel like the jerk he is, I false-started twice—yes, two times—and was disqualified and then—oh, I'm not proud—I cried and blew chunks right there by the track. I did. Vomited. And then…drum roll…it was all over.

Ken Johnson whispered "Head case."

A couple other seniors whispered "Squirrel Nuts," for that was my nickname with the upper classes.

Coach Knautz said, "Another year of experience and that won't happen to you, my boy."

Gus showed up outside the locker room and said, "You should quit stupid track because it's foolish and dumb," because track made it so I didn't have time to drive around with him and Peter Yang. He didn't have to say that, by the way. Track was done for me for the year.

And Cody Frederick said, "We'll kick ass come fall, Reinstein."

For the next five days, I stayed home. I didn't go to school because I was wrecked by the false starts. I didn't barf anymore, but I felt sick. I felt sweaty. I couldn't eat. I couldn't rest. Moist sheets. Disgusting. Didn't smell good. Jerri paced around the house all day while I lay there. She only stopped pacing to stare at me (or to go be a crossing guard for an hour). By day six, I was pretty hungry, so I ate a couple of bagels.

And that was that. No more track. Sophomore year was almost over. Summer was almost here.

While track was going, I felt I had a reason for getting out of my bed: Beat Ken Johnson. Without track, I was back to lying in bed wondering if I'm funny. (I really wanted to be a comedian…maybe I still do.)

CHAPTER 3: PROOF OF WHY I SHOULDN'T BE A COMEDIAN

A.

Nobody laughed at my jokes except for Gus, who is my best friend. He thinks I'm hilarious, of course, but he's been my best friend forever, so he's biased. My so-called second best friend, Peter Yang? He never laughed at anything. What funny man would hang out with a dude who never laughs?

B.

In seventh grade, I did the school talent show, and I ripped a routine right square out of my *Jerry Seinfeld Live on Broadway: I'm Telling You for the Last Time* DVD and nobody laughed. Jerry Seinfeld is hilarious. He's a comic genius. Everybody laughs at him. I did his shtick, and I got nothing except for Ben Schilling shouting at me to get off the stage (yes, he got detention) and also a couple of other kids booing. That means the bearer of the jokes wasn't funny (I was the bearer, if you didn't get that).

C.

When I talked, I often talked way too fast, sometimes so fast I even annoyed myself (not to mention
others), especially when I talked too fast in my head,
which, for most of my life, I have done 24/7, which is
not funny. This can still be a problem. *Shut up, voice in
head*. Not funny! Not funny! Seriously, not funny.

• • •

Let us address some larger issues, shall we?

My dad must be part of this discussion:

I used to think about my dad a lot. I used to think
he was with me wherever I went, and that made me feel
good. I used to ask him for help and ask him to keep
me safe, which is weird. He's dead. I thought a ghost
was keeping an eye on me.

Aha! When I was eleven, it occurred to me that he
killed himself (I found him when I was five), so he obviously didn't want to be with me at all because he made
sure he'd never see me again no matter what, so I stopped
kidding myself that my dad's ghost was hanging around
taking care of me. Hanging around is a bad way to put it.

Ha-ha.

See? None of that's funny.

• • •

Let's address the bonfire.

There really aren't any pictures of Dad left because when I was seven, Jerri had this giant bonfire to help me and Andrew "let go of the past." We listened to Celtic music and burned Dad's books and shirts and photo albums, etc. Just about everything. (Not totally everything.)

You can't burn memories, Jerri. I guess you know that now.

I have some memories.

Here's a memory:

One time, when I was maybe four, Dad put me in our old Volvo station wagon (a car Jerri got rid of around the time of the bonfire, even though I screamed "Noooo!") and drove us out to the big Mound east of town (an important Mound). I sat down at the bottom while Dad jogged up and down it, which doesn't make a lot of sense given what I knew about Dad from Jerri (a short, fat dad). He jogged, and I played in the dirt or whatever, and he jogged, and I remember shouting at him, "Daddy! Daddy!" etc., and he jogged. When he stopped, he was all sweaty, and he walked over to me and whispered, "That's better. That's better." Then he said, "What the hell are you doing, Felton?" I believe I was eating a rock. I remember the Volvo smelled funny on the drive back because he was so sweaty. Not exactly like Cody Frederick funny but sort of. When we got home, Dad said, "Thanks for accompanying me, buddy." That was nice.

I really loved that car—it was freaking huge—but Jerri said it had bad vibes. So it went away like all Dad's pictures.

I do have some memories though. Not funny ones.

• • •

Let's delve into Jerri a bit!

While I was home from school sweating and not eating after my Regionals screw-up, Jerri, between her crossing guard shifts, often stood at the landing of the stairs that lead into the basement, where my room is and where I watch TV. She would stand there and watch me sleeping. Except, I wasn't asleep. I was watching Comedy Central. I would pretend to sleep when I'd hear her creep down the stairs so I wouldn't have to talk to her (as she had taken to saying very weird things, very incomprehensible things that my brain did not understand). I'd squint my eyes so they looked closed, but they were open just enough to continue watching Comedy Central. Sometimes, she'd stand there looking at me for a whole episode of *MADtv*, and I'd get uncomfortable and want to move, but I didn't because her freakiness was freaking me out. Sometimes, I could hear her swallowing, like she was crying or something, which was totally weird. I got disqualified from a stupid track meet, for God's sake. I was pretty upset, but it wasn't so tragic that my mom should've been crying about it.

You know what? Of course she wasn't crying about the track meet. I was just a dumb kid back in May.

One day, she stood there for like an hour, swallowing and staring, and it just got to be too much. I had an itch on my leg and couldn't hold on anymore, so I said, "Can I help you, Jerri?"

She flinched and said, "No…just checking on you."

"Okay!" I said.

"I don't think it's bad to be in sports, Felton."

Why the hell would it be? Incomprehensible!

Then she went upstairs.

Incomprehensible jokes aren't funny, by the way.

• • •

And, finally, let's address Bluffton.

Disclaimer: Jerri says I shouldn't say "retard" all the time because it's disrespectful to people who have really low IQs, but that's not what I'm talking about, you know? I sincerely apologize to anyone I offend by saying "retard." Okay: There have been times when I truly feel like I'm a retard and that everybody thinks I'm retarded, and because they think I'm retarded, I get nervous and I act like a retard, which simply fulfills their expectations. It's a big circle. The retarded circle of my life.

Am I retarded? Well...

I am a Reinstein. I live on the outskirts of a small town in southwestern Wisconsin on ten acres from which I can see the town's little country club and golf course—which I've called ugly. From my home, I can also see all the alcoholic, blithering golf dads who swear and scream.

I blamed my dad for this situation, for abandoning us here by hanging himself in the garage. And I also blamed Jerri because she's from here and should've known better. I believe Bluffton, Wisconsin, is a terrible place.

On good days, this is what I've thought: I'm not retarded. Bluffton is retarded. It has a dumb little college, which is why my dad came here (to teach). Mostly all the students at the dumb little college are dumb, and they think they're king shit or whatever because they're drunk and walking around shouting and in college. Other than the college, Bluffton has a dumb main street, where kids my age stand around staring at each other, or, if they're old enough and have access to a car, they drive up and down the street, staring at the dumb kids staring at each other. Sometimes, they drive to Walmart, which is really big. Bluffton also has a McDonald's and a Subway and a Pizza Hut and a combo KFC–Taco Bell. (KenTacoFrickinBell—retarded.) And there are lots of hills and lots of farms outside the city limits and lots of farmers who drive their pickup trucks and smell like poop and lots of black and white cows standing on the hills staring at you like you're a retard or like you're a kid on main street.

And listen to this: I never even minded cows. I never minded poop-smelling farmers, even though they can be mean and gross (they blow snot out of their noses onto the snow). Farmers and their poop-smelling kids are not why Bluffton has seemed retarded and why me and my friends have called it Suckville.

Me, Peter, and Gus (my only friends forever) figured the facts out in eighth grade. The reason we wanted to rename Bluffton *Suckville* is because of the town kids: the public school teachers' kids and the lawyers' kids and the doctors' kids and the cops' kids and the insurance salespeople's and the bankers' kids and the orthodontist's daughter, Abby Sauter, who has been very mean.

"They're all dumb and annoying!" we shouted. "They're the retarded ones!" we said. They honestly do think they're the special children of God. Gus calls these kids honkies. I don't know why, but it makes me laugh. Even now. Honkies.

We aren't honkies (maybe I am). Me, Peter, and Gus are college kids (that is, kids of college professors).

At least, I used to be.

We are a minority! We are oppressed!

At least, I used to be. I'm crazy.

Gus and I tried to write a horror movie script last year titled *The Retarded Honkies of Suckville!* We wrote two pages actually. Gus wrote some good jokes.

I didn't write any jokes because I wasn't funny.

Gus is hilarious. Gus could be a great standup comic right now, even though he doesn't want to be. He's really small, and he's got this wad of black hair that's always sort of long, and he ducks his head so his bangs cover his eyes so he can hide the fact that he thinks everybody is just dumb. I know he's under his hair rolling his eyes and making faces. Everybody else knows too. He used to drive the junior and senior honkies crazy because they knew he was making fun of them, but they couldn't catch him because his hair wad was in front of his eyes. He's so dang funny, hugely hilarious, which is the greatest compliment I can give anybody.

He also left for the summer, which threatened to make Bluffton double Suckville, maybe triple Suckville, as I wasn't exactly in love with Peter Yang, who was my remaining friend.

Not funny. Not funny. Not funny.

A comedian? I don't think so.

• • •

It's 1:20 a.m. I am not sleepy.

ABOUT THE AUTHOR

Growing up, Geoff Herbach was both dork and jock. Sports calmed him. People caused him anxiety. Off season, Geoff was prone to kummerspeck, which is a German word meaning weight gain due to nervous eating. Its literal translation is grief bacon. Geoff teaches writing at Minnesota State, Mankato. Visit him at geoffherbach.com.